HOT S

A COLLECTION C
STORIES

Liah Wilder

Want to read more steamy short stories for free? Click here to get free access to the first few stories I wrote in 2022 plus the stories I wrote for other Medium publications during 2021.

Here's a little taste of the steamy fiction you can find in this story:

I slam down on him, taking him completely inside me with a single movement. We both moan, breaking the kiss.

He holds me by the hips as I star rocking on top of him, moving up slowly, just to slam down again, harder and faster.

I groan at the feeling of his cock stretching my pussy.

"You're so fucking tight," he whispers.

Suddenly, he grabs me by the waist, before rolling with me in the bed, so he's now the one on top.

Kevin takes one of my nipples into his mouth, sucking. He thrusts into me harder, and I let out a strangled scream, as pleasure takes over me again.

I hold on to his shoulders while he keeps sucking my nipple and thrusting into me faster and harder with every movement.

- Fucking My Boyfriend's Brother

Testing my Husband's New Handcuffs on a Stranger while Shopping

I walk past the stores until I reach the one I'm looking for. Tomorrow is my wedding anniversary, and I need something special for my husband.

I get into the sex shop, glancing at the toys. I might need some new toys soon, but today I'm looking for something else.

The maid's suit dress gets my attention, and I approach it, feeling it in my fingers.

The quality is good, but I need something else.

I run my fingers through the dresses until I find a police dress.

"That one has a matching service cap and handcuffs," the man being the counter tells me. "Would you like to see them?"

I smile at him. "Yes, please."

I take the dress and approach the counter. He handles me the cap and the handcuffs. I take them, wondering if they're good enough for what I have in mind.

"They're good quality," he tells me. "I have the same set and they haven't broken yet."

I look at him. "Well, that depends how much use you give them."

He gives me an amused look. "You can test them, and if you're not satisfied with their resistance, I'll give another set."

I nod. My attention changes to the police dress. I hold it in front of me, trying to decide if it will fit me.

"You can try it in the back if you want."

I glance at him, trying to decide what to do. I smile as the idea occurs to me.

"Thanks," I say as I follow to the back with the dress.

I put the dress on, watching in the mirror how it fits into my body, revealing my long legs and pressing my breasts together.

Opening the door, I take a peek to see if he's still alone in here. Walking back to the counter, I turn in my heels.

He gives a good look at my body, taking in my barely covered butt and pussy, and my breasts almost jumping out of my cleavage.

"I think I want to try those handcuffs now," I tell him, unzipping the dress slowly.

He follows my movement with a serious expression. Finally, he reacts.

Closing the front door, he changes the sign to *I'll be back in five.*

"You won't be back in five," I tell him, taking the handcuffs from his hands.

"We'll see," he replies defiantly.

I push him towards the back room.

I close the door after me. When he turns to face me, I use the handcuffs on him, keeping his arms away from his waist.

He looks at me with an amused smile.

"Now what?"

I run my fingers across his chest.

"Now let's play," I say, as I start to unbutton his shirt.

My fingers touch his muscular body, brushing over his hard nipples. I lean close to him, my mouth a few inches away from his.

He tries to kiss me, but I move away before he can touch my lips.

I lick his neck, kissing his soft skin and smelling his masculine scent.

My hands rest on his jeans, while I kiss his chest, running my tongue over his nipples, before going down to his stomach.

I kneel between his legs, as he presses against the handcuffs before closing his eyes with a sigh.

Unzipping his jeans, I free his already hard cock. Taking it with one hand, I hold him as I lick the tip, tasting his salty pre-cum.

He moans. I look up to his face and see his head fall back as I stroke him with my hand while the other cups his balls.

Seeing him in this situation, handcuffed and surrounded by my will makes me horny. I reach down to my wet pussy, feeling my folds with a moan.

My tongue caresses the length of his cock before I take him into my mouth. He's so big that he doesn't fit completely, and soon he's hitting the back of my throat, making me gag.

He pulls the handcuffs again, but they resist. Moving his hips, he thrusts into my mouth, matching my rhythm as my head bobs up and down his dick.

I keep caressing my pussy, my fingers touching my clit softly in a circular motion, bringing me closer to the climax.

I slip two fingers inside me, and start ducking my cunt at the same rhythm I'm sucking this stranger's dick.

He thrusts into my mouth harder, his tip hitting my throat again. I stay like that until my eyes start to water and my head becomes light.

I let him slip out of my mouth as I catch my breath, before sucking him again.

"Yes, just like that, suck me," he says between moans, his eyes closed.

I do as he says and feels his cock swelling in my mouth as he spills his seed into my mouth.

I swallow eagerly, as my fingers keep caressing my clit, and I come with an explosive orgasm.

He looks down at me, his breath is erratic.

"Fuck, that was hot."

I stand, remove the police dress, and start dressing the clothes I had when I came into the store.

He's still handcuffed, and I see him glance at his wrists before pulling on them.

I smile. "You're right. They're good."

He smiles too. "Well, will you open them?"

I play with the keys in my fingers, giving him a defiant look.

"Humm, yeah, I guess I have to if I want to take them home with me."

I free his hands, and we both go to the counter so I can pay for my police dress.

"You know what," he says when I hold out my card for him. "You can keep all this."

I shake my head. "I didn't do it for that."

He smiles, giving me a bag with my things. "I don't care. There's no way I'm gonna charge someone who decided to test my stuff on me."

I'm still taken aback, but I take the bag.

"So, that was a first?"

He nods. "I can't wait to see what you'll buy next."

When I got home and told my husband everything, he took a pen and paper and made a list of everything I should buy. And made me promise to buy everything one at a time.

A Hotwife's Date With The New Neighbor

I laugh as John makes a joke. He's not that funny, but I don't care.

I've seen him over the fence that connects our houses. He was fucking some woman's brain out on the pool. That's when I decided I wanted some too.

Allan has been gone for three months, and John moved next door a couple of weeks ago, so he doesn't know I'm married. Allan on the other hand knows what I'm up to, and likes to know all the dirty details.

I run my hands across my neck, watching how his eyes drop to my chest, following my movement.

"What if get out of here?" I ask him, playing with my necklace.

He nods, smiling.

"My place of yours?"

I give him a devilish smile. "Why not the bathroom?"

He looks at me surprised, but his eyes quickly become full of desire.

"You want me so badly that you can't wait?"

I lean forward, taking his hand between mine under the table, I pull it to my leg.

"Why wait, when we can have fun here and back at home?"

He caresses my leg, his hand moving up my dress.

I stand, smiling. Without a word, I walk to the bathroom.

I wait for him to follow me, and when I see him, I pull him into the lady's bathroom, locking the door.

I rest against the wooden door, and reach for him, pulling him into me, and kissing him.

He kisses me back, his tongue dancing with mine, as he feels my tits through my dress.

John caresses my hard nipples, breaking the kiss.

"You're not wearing a bra," he whispers in a husky voice.

I reach for his pants, unzipping them. "You should check my panties."

He gives me a wild look, before running his fingers down my body. He pulls my dress up to my waist, revealing my naked body.

I take his cock in my hand, feeling his length, as my hand moves up and down.

He groans, resting his hands on the door while I kneel in front of him.

I lick his tip, tasting his salty pre-cum, before taking him slowly into my mouth.

He lets out a sharp breath, as my head bobs up and down his shaft, and he reaches for my head, tracing the rhythm.

I gag when he starts thrusting into my throat, and my eyes become watery.

"Yeah, suck me, just like that," he whispers, thrusting into my throat again.

I reach for his balls, playing with them as I keep sucking as deep as I can.

My fingers move slowly to his hole, but he stops me when he realizes what I'm about to do.

Pulling me to my feet, he turns me around, pressing me against the door.

"You like ass play? Let's see," he whispers in my hear.

His hands across my body, while he kisses and licks my neck.

My head falls forward, resting against the door, while he pinches my nipples, making me moan.

His fingers move down my body, slipping between my legs.

"Open up," he commands, forcing my legs open.

I bite my lower lip to stop my scream when he caresses my clit in a circular motion,

"You're so wet. You like giving head?" He thrusts his fingers inside me, while his thumb presses against my throbbing bud. "Answer me, do you like sucking dick?"

I nod, moaning when he starts moving his fingers faster.

"Yeah, you do," he removes his fingers, and I feel his tip against my pussy as he enters me with a thrust.

"Oh, God," I moan, as he starts thrusting into me faster.

He slaps my ass, first one side, then the other, and I let out a whimper.

I've never been slapped before, but this only makes me hornier.

He caresses the pained areas, before moving his fingers closer to my hole.

I gasp when he teases me with his finger, pressing into me while his dick fucks me harder.

"Oh, yes," I moan, pressing against him, trying to get him deeper inside me.

"You do like ass play," he says between groans, biting my neck. "You're so tight."

Suddenly, someone tries to open the door, and John stops ducking me for a couple of seconds.

Without waiting, I move my hips towards him, until I feel his dick move in and out of me again.

"Fuck, you're a frisky one," he says, grabbing my hips and slamming into me.

He traces his rhythm, taking me close to my orgasm as his finger keeps teasing my ass while his shaft moves inside me.

"John, oh, John, just like that," I scream while the waves of pleasure take over me.

My pussy clenches around his dick as I come, taking him over the edge too.

He lets out a loud groan, slamming into me one last time, spilling his seed inside me.

John moves away from me, and I adjust my clothes with trembling fingers.

When I turn to face him, he's zipping his jeans.

A knock on the door startles us before I can say anything.

I look at my image in the mirror, before turning to the door.

I look back at him, to make sure he's dressed.

"Well, this is gonna be fun," I say, opening the door.

The manager stares at me with an annoyed look, before seeing John behind me.

He opens his mouth, but he never says anything, shocked.

I pat him on the shoulder as I walk past him.

"Maybe next time you can join us."

I hear John chuckle as we walk away from the building without looking back.

When we get outside, our eyes met and we laugh.

"You're a sweet little devil, aren't you?" He asks me.

I shrug. "So, your place or mine?"

My Husband Catches Me Showing a Good Time to Our New Neighbor, and Then Joins Us

I watch while the new neighbors take their things into their house. They bought the house a couple of weeks ago and for the looks of it, they couldn't wait to move in. For the last two days, the street has been filled with moving trucks and people taking their things into their new place.

I haven't met them yet, but from what I could see from my window, the husband is as hot as hell.

That's why I'm looking out through the windows, to catch a glimpse of his muscular body while he takes their heavy stuff into the house. He's not wearing a shirt, and the sweat shines on his tanned skin.

I bite my lower lip as I see him walk into the house again, his butt hugged perfectly by his jeans.

I can't stop wondering how amazing it must feel to have him take me into his arms, pin me against a wall and fuck me raw.

A small whimper escapes my lips as my hands travel across my body until I'm caressing my sensitive nipples through the fabric of my thin dress. I'm not wearing a bra, and my nipples immediately react to the attention while I imagine it's my new neighbor caressing me.

I feel my pussy getting wet as I keep playing with my nipples, moaning when I see my neighbor come outside again.

Suddenly, he stops in his tracks, staring straight into my house. Is he staring at me? Can he see me?

He adjusts his pants over his cock, before turning to his wife.

She looks mad.

With my heart beating fast, I move away from the window.

Laugh runs through me as I realize what just happened.

11

Well, I guess having a good relationship with them is now out of question. At least for the wife.

After what happened, I make my best to stay away from the windows. I even skip my usual jog at the end of the day. I don't want to face my neighbors yet.

I make sure dinner is almost ready for when Chris, my husband arrives. He works too much and I like to surprise him once in a while with something special.

A knock on the door startles me, and I open the front door without thinking.

My new neighbor stands in front of me with a mug in his hands. He smiles, running his hands through his hair.

"Hi! I'm Jonathan. I just moved to the house across the street," he says, holding out his hand to me.

I give him a handshake, feeling the heat run through my body at his touch.

"I'm Sarah, welcome to the neighborhood," my voice sounds off as I try to calm my heartbeat at his closeness.

"I was wondering if you could borrow me some sugar?" He asks, showing me the mug in his hand.

I nod, moving away from the door. "Yes, of course, please come inside."

He follows me to the kitchen. I feel his eyes on my body as I walk.

"My wife is working nights this week, and I just feel like having something sweet. She doesn't want me to have sugar, so I need to enjoy it when she's not home."

I turn to face him, my eyes traveling across his muscular body.

"If I were your wife I would let you have anything you want," I tell him, without thinking.

I see the fire in his eyes as he steps closer to me, leaving the mug on the counter.

"Maybe that's because you don't know what I want," he replies in a whisper as he reaches for my hair, locking it behind my ear.

I shiver at his touch and bite my lower lip.

"Maybe we want the same thing," I say, looking him in the eyes.

My heart beats fast as he leans closer to me, brushing his lips to mine. With a whimper, I pull Jonathan closer to me, kissing him.

He doesn't react at first. Suddenly, I'm worrying that maybe I misunderstood what was happening.

I move away from him, but before I can say anything, he pulls me into his arms, kissing me deeply.

I moan against his lips, as he presses his hard body against mine. I feel his cock on my stomach, my pussy becoming wet with the expectation of having him inside me.

His hands travel down my body, until he reaches my butt, squeezing and pulling me o him.

I break the kiss with a whimper.

Jonathan kisses my chin, going down to my neck. He licks and nibbles at my sensitive skin taking my earlobe into his mouth, sucking.

I moan again, lost in pleasure.

I've been fantasizing about him since the first time I've seen him, but I never expected he'll make me feel this good.

I caress his chest through his shirt, feeling his muscular body contract at my touch. Without a second thought, I pull the thin fabric, ripping it in two.

He moves away from my neck, looking down at his shirt with surprise before smirking.

"You ow me a new shirt."

I smile. "Maybe I can find a way to pay you back."

I kneel in front of him, pulling his belt and unzipping his jeans. His dick springs free in front of my eyes.

I take him in my hands, feeling his weight. I need to use both my hands to cover him completely.

Jonathan moans, resting against the wall behind him when I lick his tip. Spitting on him, I use my hands to caress him, stroking his wood eagerly, and feeling him grow in my hands.

With my eyes locked on his face, I take him slowly into my mouth, watching his expression change to pure pleasure.

He groans, holding my head in place as he starts fucking my mouth, making me gag as his tip hits the back of my throat.

"God, yeah, suck me, just like that," he whispers as my eyes become watery. "Good girl."

His praise makes me eager to please him, and I suck on him harder, bobbing my head on his cock and trying to take as much of him inside my mouth as possible.

The salty taste of his pre-cum makes me wish he would come into my mouth. I want to swallow his cum.

Suddenly, he pulls me away from his cock, making me stand.

I let out a small protest, but he shuts me up with a hard kiss on my lips.

Breaking the kiss, he makes me turn my back to him before he shoves me against the wall.

I rest my hands next to my face and lift my ass towards him, opening my legs.

He caresses my back slowly, before slapping my butt hard.

I jump, surprised.

"Don't move," he says, hitting me again.

The pain quickly turns into pleasure when he pulls my dress up to my waist, revealing my naked butt, and caresses the pained area.

He kneels between my legs, kissing the place he hit, before slipping his fingers between my folds.

I moan, biting my lower lip at the feeling.

"You're so fucking wet," he whispers.

"She likes the pain," I hear Chris replying. "Hey babe," he adds, approaching me and kissing me.

I look back at Jonathan to see his confused expression. He looks like he's about to run away.

I press my ass against him. "Don't stop what you're doing," I tell him.

His eyes are still glued on Chris.

My husband laughs. "Go ahead man, I'll just watch."

Chris moves back to a chair, sitting close to us, and taking his cock in his hands.

I moan when Jonathan licks my pussy, pressing the tip of his tongue against my clit.

Chris strokes his cock faster as my moans become lauder with the pleasure Jonathan is giving me with his tongue and his fingers.

Finally, the pleasure is too much for me, and I come hard against his mouth, with a strangled scream.

Without giving me time to come down from my orgasm, Jonathan stands behind me.

I hear the sound of something ripping, and look back to see him covering his dick with a condom before pressing his tip against my entrance.

He enters me with a thrust, making me moan in pleasure as he stretches my pussy, moving inside me harder and faster with every movement.

I look back at Chris, to see him smile at me while he keeps stroking his cock.

"Come over baby," I tell him between moans. "I want you to come in my mouth."

He smiles, stands, and pulls the chair closer to me, sitting again.

Jonathan moves with me while I lean into Chris' lap and take his wood into my mouth, sucking at the same rhythm Jonathan is fucking me.

Chris holds my head closer to him, making me gag as he loads his cum into my mouth without a warning.

I swallow and move my head away from his dick, but keep my hands resting on his knees while Jonathan keeps fucking me from behind.

Jonathan slips his hand in front of me, caressing my clit in circles until I'm close to another orgasm.

"Oh, fuck, just like that! I'm—" I scream as my orgasm takes over me in waves of pleasure.

With a final hard thrust, Jonathan comes too with a groan.

I fall to the floor between Chris's legs, breathing hard, while Jonathan leans against the wall trying to catch his breath.

Chris caresses my hair softly.

"That's the best welcome you ever gave me babe."

I look at him with a smile.

"I know. It was fun."

Jonathan moves, and we both turn to face him. He's staring at us confused.

"It's okay," I tell him. "Chris likes to watch."

Pounded By My Husband's New Colleague

I stare at my phone again.

Josh is late again. He could at least call me.

I'm about to put my phone away when it vibrates in my hands.

I check it. A text from Josh

Sorry babe, I got caught up with work. Will be there as soon as possible.

I sigh. This has been happening a lot lately.

I'll try not to get bored while I wait.

His reply comes in a couple of seconds.

I'm sure you'll find someone to keep you busy.

I don't reply. I prefer to do this when he's with me.

I sigh, wondering if maybe I should just go home. We can do this next weekend.

Before I can decide what to do, a tall man approaches me, leaning on my table with a charming smile.

"Did your friend forget about your date?" He asks, glancing at my phone still in my hand.

He's attractive enough to make me want to stay a little longer. I guess Josh was right and I've just found someone to keep me busy.

"Yeah, it's always the same with her," I lie.

Usually, when I tell the guys I'm married they run away, and that's not what I want.

He takes next to me.

"Well, lucky me," he holds out his hand to me. "I'm Trent."

I take his hand with mine, giving him a handshake, feeling the electricity running through my body at his touch. "I'm Julie." Another lie.

He leans closer to me, brushing his leg on mine as he talks about banal things.

I'm not paying attention to anything he's saying. All I can think about is how close he is, and how much I want to take him to the restroom right now.

Trent's hand finds my leg, and he looks at me looking for my reaction, but I simply smile as he keeps talking.

His hand slips up my leg, caressing my skin, and I open my legs softly letting him feel my bare pussy.

Trent keeps making circles with his hand on my leg, brushing my folds gently.

My pussy becomes wet, and I let out a small moan, wanting more.

Unable to keep this up, I hold his hand still on my leg.

"Maybe we should get out of here," I tell him.

"My place or yours?" He whispers in my ear.

I shake my head. "I was thinking about something closer, like the restroom."

He's surprised at first, but then his expression changed, and he nods with a devilish smile.

Trent follows me into the ladies' bathroom, and I close the door after him, before turning to face him.

He takes a step towards me, and I kill the remaining distance between us, kissing him passionately.

Trent kisses me back, resting his hands on my waist and pulling me closer to him.

I feel his fingers slip under my dress, caressing my legs, and traveling to my center of pleasure.

Opening my legs, I give him access. A moan escapes my lips when he traces my folds with his fingers.

"You're so fucking wet," he whispers against my lips before kissing me again.

His fingers circle my clit, teasing me. my legs start to shake, and I hold on to his shoulders while the pleasure he's giving me becomes all I can feel.

Slipping a finger in my pussy, Trent starts fucking me with his fingers, adding another two to the first, and taking me closer to the orgasm.

Pressing my clit with his thumb at the same time his fingers keep working their wonder on my cunt, I feel the waves of pleasure take over me, as I came with a strangled scream.

My legs are shaking, and Trent gives me a couple of minutes to stabilize before he turns me around, making me lean against the door.

I rest my hands on the wooden surface, at each side of my head, arching my back to him, and lifting my ass. My legs are open, and I wait for him to enter me.

I hear him tear a condom foil before covering himself.

Holding me by the hips, Trent aligns himself between my legs.

I open up wider, giving him better access to my pussy.

He runs his tip through my folds, pressing softly against my entrance before moving again, teasing me.

All I want is to have him inside me, and here he is, teasing me and refusing me what I need.

"Just fuck me already!" I tell him, unable to keep waiting.

He lets out a soft chuckle against my neck giving me goosebumps.

"That's what I wanted."

With these words, I feel his tip pressing against my pussy again, but this time he enters me slowly until he's completely buried inside me.

We both let out a moan as he starts moving in and out of me. Trent moves slowly at first, increasing his rhythm with every thrust until he's fucking me hard and fast.

Just the way I like it.

My moans fill the restroom, while he keeps moving in and out of me faster.

I start moving back, meeting his thrusts and making him fuck me deeper.

"Oooh, just like that, yes!" My voice sounds broken as I breathe hard and moan with his thrusts.

Suddenly moving out of me, Trent makes me turn around.

He kisses my lips eagerly before taking me by the waist, lifting me from the floor. I wrap my legs around him, feeling his hard dick pressing against my wet pussy while he walks with me to the counter.

I barely feel the cold stone under my butt against my sensitive skin before he pulls me to the edge and enters me with a thrust.

I moan again, holding him by his shoulders. My legs pull him into me, while he keeps slamming down on me, my pussy stretching at his size.

I feel my orgasm approaching me again. My head falls back, and he kisses my neck, moving down to my chest.

One of my hands moves to my breast, teasing my hard nipple before pulling down the thin fabric of my dress.

Trent pulls my nipple into his mouth, sucking hard before biting gently.

Waves of pleasure take over me as I come again, this orgasm stronger than the first one.

My pussy clenches around his cock, and I feel him trembling.

Moving away from him, I jump down from the counter and make him lean on it before I kneel in front of him.

He removes his condom, looking at me defiantly. I smile, licking my lips.

My hand moves to his wood, stroking him gently at first.

He lets out a groan, and I watch as his head falls back and he loses himself with pleasure.

I lick his tip, tasting his salty pre-cum, before lowering my mouth into his cock, sucking hard.

I move my head up and down his shaft, taking him eagerly into my mouth, teasing him with my tongue, and sucking until his tip hits the back of my throat, making me gag.

His hand holds my head, keeping me in place as he starts thrusting into my mouth with the same rhythm he was fucking my pussy.

I'm struggling to breathe when he lets go of my head, letting me breathe before slamming down on my throat again.

My hands play with his balls feeling their weight and teasing him.

"Fuck, that's it!" He roars, realigning his load down my throat.

Some of it spills down my chin, but I collect it with my fingers, sucking on them while he watches.

"Damn, that was hot," he whispers, holding out his hand to me and helping me stand.

I smile, checking my image in the mirror and rearranging my clothes.

When I look back at him, Trent is already at the door.

"Should I go first?" He asks.

I shake my head. "We can just get out together."

I follow him out of the restroom, and when we reach the bar, I see that Josh has finally arrived.

I'm ready to say goodbye to Trent when to my surprise he walks toward Josh.

"Hey, here you are!" He says with a smile. "I hope you haven't been waiting for too long."

Josh looks from Trent to me. He knows what we were doing.

"No, I just got here."

Trent turns to face me.

"Oh, I'm so rude," he says. "This is ..."

"Clara, my wife," Josh says in an amused tone. "Honey, Trent is the new colleague I've talking about."

I see Trent's expression changing as he realizes that I lied to him, giving him a fake name.

"What?"

I approach Josh and give him a small kiss on the lips.

"Hey, babe. You were right, I found someone to keep me busy. I'll tell you all about it when we get home."

I watch as my words sink in and Trent realizes what's happening.

I'm a hotwife.

I Bet With My Husband That Would Fuck The New Pool Guy Before The End of His First Week

"The pool guy will be here in a couple of minutes," my husband tells me with a smirk.

I know what it's trying to say, but I stay silent.

He walks to the door. "I'll be at work."

I smile, accepting the challenge. "I'll tell you all about it when you come back."

He shakes his head. "I bet him on fall for it."

I take a step closer to him, kissing him on the lips. "I bet when you return, I'll taste like his cum."

Jeffrey laughs, shaking his head again and leaving the house.

I get into my bedroom, looking for the skimpiest bikini I have. Finally, I find a red bikini that barely covers my body.

With a smile, I go down to the pool, resting on one of the chairs while I wait.

It doesn't take long before I hear the back gate open.

I jump out of my chair, and my hat flies into the water.

"Oh. Fuck!"

I try to reach it, kneeling on the floor next to the pool.

"Mrs. Cameron, can I help you?"

I look back in time to see Sean checking out my butt in the air as I try to reach the hat.

"That would be great," I tell him, turning to face him, without standing.

My face is right at the height of his cock, and I see him blush as he removes his shirt and jumps into the pool.

He surfaces with my hat in his left hand, approaching me with a victorious smile.

"There you have," he says.

I reach out to take it from his hands, but end up falling into the pool, right into Sean's arms.

He holds me against his body, and I feel his hard cock pressing on my hip.

"Are you okay?" He asks.

I nod, pressing harder against his cock. "I'm great."

Without a second thought, I run my hands across his chest, until they're resting on his shoulders. I lean closer to him, taking his lips with mine, and kissing him passionately.

He kisses me back, his tongue dancing with mine as we explore each other's mouths.

I feel his hands on my lower back before Sean presses me harder against his muscular body.

I'm lost in pleasure when I feel his dick pressing against me. Reaching between our bodies, I slip a hand down to his cock, stroking him gently.

He moans against my lips as I keep caressing him through the thin fabric of his swim shorts.

His hands move up my body, caressing my soft skin until he's touching under my breasts.

I let out a soft moan, as my body shakes in anticipation.

He grabs my breast, teasing my nipple through my bikini, before pulling it aside and flinching the hard bud with his thumb.

A noise in my neighbor's backyard interrupts us, and we look at each other breathing hard. I take his hand from my breast, covering myself again.

I know Mr. Beaver likes to watch Jeffrey and me having sex, but today it's not his lucky day.

"Let's go inside," I tell Sean, before kissing him.

I bite his lower lip, before getting out of the pool and taking him inside with me.

As soon as we're inside, I turn to face him, throwing myself at him. My lips cover his, as my hands travel down his body, to his hard cock.

He moans against my lips, and I kneel in front of him with a smile.

"Oh, fuck!" He whispers as I pull down his swimming shorts.

His cock springs free in my face, and I bite my lower lip while I take him in my hand. I stroke him gently, before licking the salty pre-cum from his tip.

One of my hands grabs his base while the other one teases his balls, and I take his cock in my mouth.

Sean starts shaking and I stop immediately, afraid that he would come this fast.

I look up at him, surprised. "Is this your first blowjob?" I ask.

Jeffrey told me that Sean is in college, so I was expecting someone with some experience.

He shakes his head, clearly embarrassed. "No."

I give up on the subject and refocus on the hard cock in front of me.

I take it in my mouth again, sucking gently at first, determined to give him something to talk about.

He closes his eyes as I keep sucking, my head bobbing up and down his cock.

I gag when his tip hits my throat, making him groan.

Suddenly, he pulls me away from his cock, and I look up surprised.

"I was enjoying that," I tell him with a pouty smile.

He smiles back, grabbing my arm and making me stand.

"You'll enjoy what's next more."

Kissing me, his tongue plays with mine as his fingers caress my skin.

Sean finds my nipples, moving my bikini away from the sensitive buds, and he takes one into his mouth, sucking.

I moan as my head falls back and my fingers run through his hair, pulling him into me.

His hand moves down my body, caressing my stomach and finding my bikini bottoms.

Sean caresses my pussy over the thin fabric before untying the loop from both sides and letting the fabric fall to the floor.

I open my legs, giving him better access to my center of pleasure as he teases me with his fingers.

He feels my folds gently making me moan while his mouth keeps teasing the other nipple, giving it the same attention as the first one.

His thumb presses against my clit, and I let out a strangled scream.

"Fuck, that feels so good," I barely recognize my voice.

He throws me on the couch right when my legs start shaking and moves between them.

I open up wide, so he can kneel between my legs. I let out a deep breath as his mouth pressed against my wet pussy.

I close my eyes, arching my back as his mouth kisses my sensitive area.

Sean's tongue runs between my folds. A loud moan escapes my lips when he sucks my clit at the same time his fingers slip inside me.

He takes me over the edge with his mouth and his fingers until I'm trying to pull him away from me. I'm too close to coming.

My climax takes over me and I scream, pressing my legs against his head.

He holds me tight and keeps caressing my clit with his tongue as I ride my orgasm.

I'm barely aware of him removing his clothes when I feel the tip of this dick at my entrance before he enters me, slowly.

Sean stops before slamming down on me and filling me.

Our eyes meet and I see his trying to control himself.

I let out a loud moan and wrap my legs around him, pressuring him to start moving.

Slowly, he moves out of me just to slam down back inside me, harder and faster. He's quick to catch a good rhythm, fucking me as hard as he possibly can, and taking me close to another orgasm.

I feel the waves of pleasure taking over me again as he teases my clit with his fingers while his dick moves inside me, stretching my pussy.

My orgasm takes over me as I scream in pleasure. My pussy wrapping around his cock takes him over the edge and the comes too with a roar in my ear.

He collapses on top of me, breathing hard.

Suddenly, the front door flies open and Jeffrey enters the room.

Sean jumps away from me, his eyes glancing from me to Jeffrey. He looks embarrassed and uncomfortable.

I want to laugh. Sean doesn't know anything about our bet, and he's probably expecting Jeffrey to snap at him.

Instead, Jeffrey closes the door calmly and smiles at him.

"Did you have a good time?"

Sean looks confused before nodding slowly.

"Well, now it's time for you to get dressed and do your fucking job. Can you do that?"

Sean nods again, collecting his clothes and running away from the living room and into the back, to the pool.

I sit on the couch and laugh. "You didn't have to be that mean."

"Well, I was expecting him to at least offer some resistance. I just lost our bet."

I stand and give him a good look at my body.

"Well, are you gonna refuse this?"

He laughs, pulling me into him. "But I'm your husband."

"Yes, you are. And he just fucked me. Do you want to know the details? I thought Mr. Beaver was going to call you. He saw things getting hot in the pool."

"Someday he'll come over and try to fuck you too."

"That's a bet I'm willing to take," I tell him with a smile before taking his lips with mine.

Mr. Beaver gives me some hot sugar daddy vibes. I'll guess someday I'll have to give it a try.

Best Sex of My Life While Babysitting

I lean forward to the oven, pulling the cooking out. The smell of baked goods fills the kitchen while I smile to myself and leave the tray to rest on the counter.

I hear steps behind me and turn just in time to see Jonathan enter the room.

"Smells good," he says, approaching me.

He leans against the counter and takes a cookie from the tray before it falls from his hands.

"Ouch! It's hot!"

I shake my head. "Yes, and they're for your kids."

He laughs. "I want a cookie too."

I approach him, taking his hand with mine and blowing some hair to his fingers.

"Maybe I can get you something."

He looks down at my mouth. Licking his lips softly, I see his eyes become dark with desire.

We've been flirting for a few months now, and I've been wondering what will it take for him to make the move.

Without a second thought, I take his fingers into my mouth, my eyes locked on his while I flicked my tongue over them.

I pull his fingers out of my mouth. If this doesn't make him take me over the kitchen table, I don't know what will.

"Does it feel hot?"

He stares at me in silence.

"You can say that," he finally replies. "Where are the kids?"

"With your ex. They'll be here in an hour."

He nods slowly. I see the doubts in his eyes.

Killing the distance between us, I press myself against him. His already hard cock is against my stomach, giving me the confirmation I needed.

He wants me as much as I want him. He just needs some help deciding. And that's something I'm willing to do.

Standing on my tiptoes, I take his lips with mine, kissing him with desire. He moans and kisses me back, his tongue exploring.

His hands pull me closer to him, and my breasts press against his chest, making me shiver.

My hands caress his hair, his neck, and his shoulders, feeling his muscular body through his clothes.

Jonathan moves us until he's pressing me against the counter before he pulls me up and makes me sit next to the cookies.

My dress comes up to my hips, his hands caressing my skin, approaching slowly my pussy.

He traces a path of kisses down my neck, nibbling and licking until he reaches my cleavage. Moving down my dress and my bra, he frees my tits before he takes a nipple into his mouth, sucking.

I moan, pulling him closer to me.

He keeps teasing my nipples while his hand finds my wet panties, tracing my pussy over the thin fabric.

I move my ass to press against his hand, but he stops me.

Moving my panties to the side, his fingers trace my folds softly, making me moan.

When his finger finds my clit, caressing me in a circular motion, I gasp and bite my lips to stop the scream that's on my throat.

He moves his attention to the other nipple at the same time his fingers press against my entrance.

I open my legs wider, giving him better access to my hole.

His fingers start fucking me slowly, taking me closer to the orgasm I desperately need.

Jonathan's thumb pressing against my clit while his fingers fuck me and he sucks my nipple sends me over the edge. I climax in waves of pleasure that I can't describe.

I'm barely aware of him undressing, before his tip presses against my entrance.

Suddenly, I push him away from me and jump from the counter.

He looks at me surprised, but when I kneel in front of him, taking his cock in my hands, he closes his eyes in pleasure.

I stroke him softly before pressing my tongue to his tip, feeling his salty taste.

He moans quietly. I take his dick between my lips, sucking eagerly. I want to give him as much pleasure as he's given me.

I keep sucking while my hands play with his balls, feeling their weight.

His cock twitches on my mouth, and I feel he's close.

Before I can keep sucking him, though, he pulls me up to meet him and kisses me.

I kiss him back, before he interrupts the kiss, making me turn around.

I lean against the counter, my elbows resting on the cold stone, while he adjusts himself behind me.

"You've been driving me crazy," he says, making me open my legs for him.

I press back to him, feeling his dick against my folds and moaning.

He holds me by the hips and enters me with a thrust, making us both moan.

His large cock stretches my pussy in pleasurable pain. He stays still for a few seconds giving me time to get used to his invasion.

"I can't wait any longer. I need to fuck this hot pussy," he says, moving out of me just to slam back inside. "Fuck, you're so tight."

He keeps pounding me faster and harder every time until I feel close to my orgasm again.

I can tell he's close too by the way he's speeding his rhythm, and when his fingers find my clit, pinching me, I scream.

The waves of pleasure take over me while I reach my climax.

He comes too with a groan, pressing hard against me, and spilling his seed inside me.

Jonathan kisses my shoulder before he moves away from me softly.

I turn to face him, and the smile on his face matches mine.

"Are you okay?" He asks.

I nod. How can he ask me that? Doesn't he see my smile?

"I've been dreaming about this for a long time," I confess, arranging my clothes.

His smile grows wider.

"Me too."

The doorbell sounds before I can say anything, and the sound of his kids running into the house interrupts us.

But we talk about what happened later. And the two of us decide maybe what we feel for each other is worth the try.

So we try.

Tomorrow is my wedding day, and I couldn't be happier.

Babysitting at the Park Just Turned into Sex

I watch while the kids are with some friends. I don't know why their mom still calls me to take them to the park, they're old enough to simply sit in a corner playing on their phones with their friends while I just sit at a safe distance and watch.

They don't even move from the place they are until it's time for us to go back home.

A tall handsome man takes a seat next to me.

I smile at him. I've seen him around several times.

"Which one is yours?" He asks, looking at the toddlers.

I shake my head. "They're over there."

He follows my eyes, to the preteens.

"Wow, that old?"

I laugh. "They're not mine. I'm their babysitter. Their mom doesn't feel like it's safe for them to be outside without supervision, so here I am."

"Better safe than sorry, right?" He says.

I smile, nodding. "Sure," I look around the park. "What about your kids?"

He looks down with a smile.

"I don't have kids."

I stare at him, surprised. "Then what are you doing here?"

His hand rests on my knee, sending goosebumps through my body.

I look down at his hand, waiting for his reply.

"I've seen you around. I just felt like I should try to talk to you."

I smile. "I think that's a good call, but I'm not in the mood to talk."

I take his hand with mine and pull it up my leg a little, squeezing.

His eyes become darker with desire, as he leans closer to me.

"My car is over there, wanna check it out?"

I glance at the kids before looking at his car. I can still see the kids from there, even though I know they won't move until I make them go home.

I stand, nodding. He holds my hand, standing too, and walks me to his car.

I glance at the kids one last time before I get into the back seat, moving to the side to give him space to sit next to me.

He jumps on me the moment he closes the door, taking my lips with his.

His tongue dances with mine, exploring my mouth while he presses himself against me.

I feel his hands on my body, feeling my breasts through my tank top.

I reach down to his cock, feeling him through his jeans before unzipping them. I take his dick in my hands, stroking him.

His hand settles on my leg before going under my skirt.

I open my legs, granting him access to my pussy, and moan when he presses the wet spot in my panties.

He moves my underwear to the side, feeling my folds with his fingers before pressing his thumb to my clit.

I moan again, my head falling back on the car seat as he caresses my clit in a circular motion.

I cup his balls with my hand, feeling their weight while I tease him, making him groan.

His mouth travels down my neck, kissing my soft skin as he traces a path down to my cleavage.

He moves my tank top and my bra down to get access to my already hard nipples before pulling one into his mouth while his fingers play with the other.

I keep stroking his hard cock with my hands, giving attention to the sensitive tip and to the balls.

Leaning forward, I take his dick into my mouth, sucking hard. He groans again, thrusting into my mouth until his tip hits the back of my throat, making me gag.

My eyes sting with the effort I'm making to keep him in my mouth while gagging, and I move away to catch my breath.

He pulls me into his lap, ripping my panties with a gesture.

I straddle him, feeling his hard cock press against my pussyfoot before he makes me go down on him slowly, until he's completely inside me.

My pussy stretches, adjusting to his size, as he starts moving slowly, as if giving me time to get used to him.

I rest my hands in his shoulders, using them to support myself while I move up on his cock just to slam down on him hard.

We both moan, as I repeat the movement again.

He holds me by the hips, helping me keep a rhythm to take us both to the climax as I slam down on him harder and faster.

With every movement I make, his pelvis rubs against my clit, taking me closer to the orgasm, and when he takes one nipple into his mouth, sucking, I lose control as waves of pleasure wash over me.

He keeps thrusting into me through my orgasm, until I move from his cock to take him into my mouth again.

My head bobs up and down on his cock, as I cup his balls again, taking him to the verge of the climax.

He roars, thrusting into my mouth as he came, spilling his seed into my mouth and I swallow everything eagerly.

I move away from his cock, smiling.

He looks at me with a pleased expression.

"That was amazing," he says, caressing my shoulder.

I shrug. "You should see what I do when I'm not in a back seat."

His smile grows wider. "That sounds like a plan."

I look out the window, and realize that the kids are still in the same place where I left them.

Getting out of the car, I look at him.

"Maybe we can do this again soon, and then I'll decide if you can have more."

He tilts his head to the right. "I'll make you scream next time."

I give him a cocky smile. "Can't wait to see you trying."

With that, I close the door and go get the kids.

We fucked in the park for a few more times before I accepted to go out on a date. I fucked him in the restaurant that night. But that's a story for another day.

My Babysitting Summer Job

Sometimes you get lucky and find a job that helps you follow your dreams. My last babysitting job was one of those.

I've known the Clarkson family since I was a kid. They have four sons. Jeff is the oldest, and he's just a couple of years older than me.

I've had a crush on him since that time in high school when he helped me get to the right class.

But he ignored me after that.

The younger of the Clarksons is eight years old.

When the mom called me and asked me to babysit him, I couldn't refuse. Maybe I got lucky and managed to be around Jeff? Even in college, I can't stop thinking about him.

Well, I barely saw him that night. But destiny was on my side.

She called again, but this time she wanted me to go on vacation with them. I would spend days babysitting on the beach.

The sun, bikinis, and everything hot.

What else could I ask?

I said yes, and a plan started to form in my mind.

This would be the perfect time to try my luck with Jeff.

I watch while the younger kids play on the sand, making sure they're safe.

Footsteps next to me startle me, and I look up from the place where I'm laying, to see Jeff sitting by my side.

"What's up?" He asks, his eyes traveling down my body.

I'm wearing a small bikini that shows more than hides. His eyes stop at my hard nipples, pressing against the thin fabric that's covering them.

I shrug. "You know. Working."

He smiles, looking at my lips. "This got to be the best job someone can have. Laying on the beach and getting tanned at the same time you work . . ." His eyes fall to my chest again.

I get up from my towel, suddenly offended by his words.

"Well, you know what's even better? Not having to work at all."

I grab my things and walk toward the other kids.

"Hey, guys, what if we go get an ice cream?"

They nod, laughing, and we all go together.

I try to stop thinking about Jeff, but my mind keeps going back to him checking me out.

That keeps me up at night, even if we don't talk again throughout the day.

I turn in my bed, trying to get some sleep, but I can't.

Finally giving up, I jump out of the bed, mad with myself, and walk down the stairs to get some water.

Why can't I stop thinking about Jeff? All he cares about is messing with me.

I get some water, and look down at the counter, resting my hands on the edge and leaning forward. My head falls, as I try to breathe.

A sound behind me startles me, and I straighten up, looking back.

Jeff stands a couple of feet away from me, staring at me as if this is the first he's seeing me.

"What are you doing?" I ask.

He shakes his head. "Sorry, I just couldn't sleep. I didn't mean to scare you."

I shrug. "You didn't scare me," I lie.

He takes a step closer.

"Don't lie to me, or I'll have to punish you."

I laugh. "I would love to see you trying."

He looks at me like a lion about to jump on its prey. Before I can react, he kills the distance between us, taking my lips with his.

I moan against his mouth, kissing him back eagerly.

I've wanted this for so long. I can't believe this is finally happening.

His hands run across my body, pulling me closer to him, and I let out a whimper when I feel his hard cock pressing against my stomach.

My fingers caress his hair, pulling him into me, and making the kiss deeper.

I feel his muscular body as I trace a path down his body, touching his chest.

I hesitate when I'm about to touch his cock. Jeff holds my hand and rests it on his bulge.

"Touch me," he whiskers, against my lips. "That's all I can think about since I've seen this sweet body of yours in that damn bikini."

All my doubts vanish at his words, and I feel him through the fabric of his boxers.

There's a wet spot where his tip is. I slip my hand inside his underwear, stroking him.

He kisses a path down my neck, to my chest, licking and nibbling at my sensitive skin.

My nipples are already hard when he brushes them with his fingertips through the thin fabric of my tank top.

Moving down my top, Jeff takes one of my nipples into his mouth, sucking and biting gently.

I let out a moan.

"You need to be silent or I'll have to get something for your mouth."

I kneel in front of him. "I think you already have something to keep my mouth busy," I replied, licking the tip of his cock.

I run my tongue down his length before returning to the sensitive tip. I take him into my mouth, sucking.

My head moves up and down his length, and I feel his tip hitting the back of my throat, making me gag.

He holds me in place through the hair and thrusts into my mouth faster and harder.

My spit runs down my chin, as I try to accommodate his cock in my mouth without success.

I gag again and he pulls me away from his cock. He sits me on the counter behind me, spreading my legs open for him, and removing my shorts and my panties with a single movement.

"I told you to be quiet."

Jeff runs the tip of his cock through my pussy, and I let out a small whimper. I need him inside me.

"You're so wet already. So fucking responsive."

He kneels between my legs, pulling them over his shoulders. The first lap of his tongue over my clit had me biting my mouth, as I try to stay silent while he keeps licking and sucking on my sensitive bud.

He slips two fingers inside me, moving them in and out of me while his mouth keeps working its wonders on my body.

I start trembling, feeling my orgasm approaching me.

Suddenly, he moves away from my cunt, leaving me wanting more.

"What—?" I say, ready to protest, but I stop when I see him aligning his cock with my entrance.

He presses against me, entering me slowly and giving me time to get used to his size.

When he's finally inside me we both moan before he starts moving.

His movements become faster and harder as he finds the rhythm that will take us both to the climax.

I let out a small cry of pleasure, and he stops.

"Be quiet or I'll have to punish you."

I look him in the eye, defiantly. "You'll have to try harder."

I gasp when he moves out of me, spinning me on the counter. He lifts my ass to him, spanking me before his cock slams down on me from behind.

He starts fucking me harder and faster, every thrust taking me closer to the orgasm.

I bite my hand to stop my screams of pleasure while he keeps pounding me harder.

The waves of pleasure take over me, sending me to the edge.

My pussy clenches around his cock, pulling him with me to the climax.

"Fuck!" He says, moving out of me and spilling his seed on my back.

I let my head fall to the counter as I try to catch my breath. I feel something soft on my back.

Jeff cleans his cum from my body with a paper towel, and I smile at him.

When he's done, he throws the towel into the garbage before pulling me into his arms.

"Are you okay?" He asks against my hair.

I nod. "I'm great," I pause for a second. "Are you okay?"

He nods, kissing my forehead. "Yes. I just can't believe this happened."

I look him in the eyes. "What do you mean?"

I smile. "I've wanted you for so long . . . I'm afraid I'll awake and realize this is just another dream."

His words warm my heart.

"You've dreamed of me?"

He nods. "Every night."

I step on my tiptoes, kissing him gently. "Me too."

Fucking My Match on My Client's Couch

The day was too long. I'm babysitting two kids for the first time, and it's a relief knowing that they're finally asleep. I would love to go home now, but checking the time, I realize their mother won't be home in at least three more hours.

She went on a date with some guy she met on a dating app.

I check my phone and decided to scroll through social media while I wait for her when I get a new notification from my favorite dating app.

The guy I was checking out while giving dinner to the kids matched me!

There's a message from him.

Hi! How are you?

I stare at my phone while my dirty mind starts getting wild. His profile says he lives a block away from here.

Maybe I could get some fun too?

I reply to his message, and we talk for a couple of minutes before I invite him to visit me.

My heart beats fast while I wonder what the hell am I doing. This isn't my place, and I'm inviting someone I just met over? What if the mom finds out? What if the kids wake up?

I'm about to message him not to come when someone knocks on the front door.

Shit! Too late. I just hope he's not a serial killer.

Taking a deep breath, I open the door. My heart skips a beat at the sight of him.

He is gorgeous, sexy, and has a hint of adventure that makes my pussy wet instantly.

"Hi! I'm Charles," he says with a smile.

I smile back at him. "Sarah."

I move away from the door to let him inside and close the door after him.

"So, what movie would you like to watch?" He asks, turning to face me.

I shrug. "You can choose," all I could think about when I invited him in was what kind of movie I would like to *make* with him.

He follows me to the living room, where my laptop rests on the couch.

I grab it before sitting down and Charles takes a seat next to me, without touching me.

We chose a movie, and rest close to each other while the movie starts.

Charles doesn't make any movement y toward me, and I'm starting to wonder if I made a mistake.

Soon he'll have to leave, and I don't want that to happen before I can get a taste of him.

Moving my hand slowly towards his leg, I caress him through his jeans.

Charles looks at me with a smile, before leaning closer to me and taking my lips with his.

I kiss him back, happy to get what I wanted, but I need more.

He leans closer to me, pressing his muscular body against mine and I moan in pleasure while my hand travels up his leg and finds the bulge on his pants.

He presses against my hand while I unzip his jeans and pull his dick out, stroking him.

He breaks the kiss, his head falling back while I keep stroking his cock with my hands.

Seeing the pleasure in his expression does something to me, and all I want is to please him.

I change positions on the couch so I can take him in my mouth, licking his tip before sucking him.

He moans, holding my head through the hair.

"Fuck that's so hot!"

I spit on him, using my hands to spread my spit on his cock before taking him in my mouth again.

I move my head up and down his size, taking in as much of him as possible.

He holds my head as he starts thrusting into my mouth, and I feel his close to an orgasm.

My hand moves to his balls, playing with them, and teasing him until he's on the verge of pleasure.

"Oh, just like that! I'm cumming!" He says a little too loud before I feel his load hit my throat.

I swallow his cum, moving away from how cock with a smile.

He looks at me with a mix of surprise and satisfaction, as he breathes hard and smiles.

"That was amazing," he says, pulling me closer to him.

"That's just the beginning," I reply.

His smile grows wider. "Good, 'cause I want to give back."

Charles makes me stand in front of him, removing my clothes until I'm naked.

I lay on the couch and he leans closer to me, kissing my lips gently before tracing a path of kisses down my neck.

He takes a nipple into his mouth, biting softly before sucking.

I moan, grabbing his head and pulling him closer to me.

He keeps biting, sucking, and licking my nipple before moving to the other one and giving it the same attention as the first one.

I arch my back in pleasure, as he moves down my stomach, licking my sensitive skin.

He opens my legs, adjusting himself between them, before lowering his head into my center of pleasure.

"You smell so good," he says before pressing his thumb against my clit.

I let out a strangled scream, almost forgetting that I need to be quiet or the kids will wake up.

His tongue caresses my folds, pressing against my entrance before moving back up and circling my clit.

I press my teeth together, closing my eyes trying to endure the pleasure he's giving me in silence.

When he slips a finger inside me, and then a second one, at the same time he sucks my clit, I gasp in pleasure.

The waves of pleasure take over me while he keeps licking and fucking me with his fingers until my legs stop shaking.

He moves away from me slowly, and I see his hard cock standing, ready for more.

Charles remove his clothes, took a condom from his wallet, and covered himself before returning to the couch.

I get on my knees, open my legs, and give him access to my pussy again.

I feel his tip pressing against my entrance before he starts moving into me slowly.

My pussy stretches at his entrance, trying to get used to his size.

I moan when he fills me, the sweet pain of his invasion making me tremble.

Charles starts moving in and out of me gently at first, speeding slowly as he tries to find the perfect rhythm that'll take us both to the climax.

I move back to meet his thrust, making him go deeper inside me.

"Faster, fuck me faster," I beg, biting the couch's arm to muffle my moans.

He holds me by the hips and starts slamming down on me harder and faster, moaning too while his dick moves inside me.

I feel his finger pressing against my asshole. This is a first for me, but something inside me just wants to let him do whatever he wants if that means I'm about to have the best orgasm of my life.

His finger enters me slowly, as he keeps pounding my pussy.

The feel of his finger moving slowly inside me while his dick fucks my cunt hard and fast intensifies the pleasure he's giving me.

"Oh, fuck!" I let out as the waves of pleasure take over me.

He keeps fucking me hard, and removing his finger from my asshole, thrusts faster into me.

Charles holds me by the hips, pulling me into him as he thrusts one last time as he reaches the orgasm with a roar.

We both collapsed on the couch,m breathing hard.

After a couple of minutes, I glance at him and see him staring at me. I let out a laugh, happy with everything that just happened between us.

"This was amazing," he says, kissing my forehead.

I nod. "I've never done something like this, you know."

"What do you mean?"

I shrug. "Having sex with someone I just met. Invite a stranger to a client's place."

He pulls me closer to him. "Well, I'm glad you did tonight."

I smile. "Yeah, me too. I just hope the kid's mom never finds out."

Turns out she did find out. The moment she got back home Charles had already left and I had cleaned the living room.

I thought I had everything managed, but the moment she checked the cameras in the garden, she knew I had company.

I lost my job that day. But I won something better.

Charles and I kept seeing each other, but we would meet at my place mostly.

We dated for a couple of years before he got an offer for his dream job.

Across the world. He left.

I almost left with him, but I couldn't.

So I stayed.

We still have some fun together when he visits, and he's still the best fuck I ever had.

Cheating on my Boyfriend with his Roommate

I stare at my phone, scrolling without paying much attention to what I'm seeing.

Glancing at my boyfriend, I see that he's starting yet another game.

Why does he invite me over it all he wants to do is play games? Am I supposed to stay here and just watch?

The seat next to me sinks when Colton takes a seat next to me. His leg brushes against mine, and I look at him.

He smiles. "Another interesting night?"

I shrug. "That's what it looks like."

He chuckles, taking my phone from my hand.

"Why don't you play with him?"

"He doesn't want me to mess with his score," I reply with disdain.

I'm a better gamer than my boyfriend, but he doesn't know because he doesn't want to play with me.

"Humm? My score is perfect!" John isn't even paying any attention to what we're saying.

I get up from the couch. "I'll just go to bed."

I wait for a few seconds for a reaction from John, but it doesn't look like he heard me at all.

Colton stands too.

"I would never let you sleep alone if I was your boyfriend," he whispers.

I feel my cheeks turning red.

Colton goes to his bedroom, and I follow him. I stop at John's door.

"Hey, Colton!" I call without thinking about what I'm doing. "What else would you do?"

He looks at me confused.

"If I was your girlfriend. What would you do?"

47

His eyes become dark with desire, while he takes in my shorts and thin tank top. I'm not wearing underwear, and my nipples are hard against my clothes.

Colton takes a step closer to me.

I take a deep breath.

He takes another step.

I want him to throw me against the wall and fuck me. Do what John won't.

Colton stops a few inches away from me. He leans forward, and I feel his breath on my neck when he talks.

"I wouldn't be playing games. I would kiss, lick and bite every inch of your sweet body until you beg me to fuck you. Then I would make you scream as you come in my cock."

My heart skips a beat at his words.

He stands a few inches from me, if I move, I'll taste his lips.

Without a second thought, I kill the distance between us, taking his mouth with mine.

He groans against my lips, pressing me against the wall while he kisses me passionately.

I kiss him back with the same passion, my hands caressing his hair, going down to his shoulders, feeling his muscular body.

His hands find my breasts, pinching my nipples through the fabric of my tank top.

I moan against his mouth. Colton pulls me into his bedroom, closing the door and pressing me against it.

His body presses against mine when he kisses me again, and I feel his hard cock on my stomach.

I reach down, feeling him through his jeans, making him moan. Unzipping his jeans, I take his cock in my hand, stroking him softly.

He groans, and pulling down my tank top, reveals my tits. Colton leans into me and takes one of my nipples into his mouth, sucking and teasing me with his tongue.

My head falls back against the door while I bite my lower lip to stop myself from moaning.

His fingers slip under my shorts, go find my pussy. I open my legs for him to have better access.

He traces my folds with his fingers before caressing my clit in a circular motion.

I keep stroking his dick, feeling him grow even bigger in my hands, and cup his balls teasing him with my fingers.

He pulls me from the door with a groan and throws me into his bed, kneeling by my side.

Colton pull my clothes from my body, making me lay naked on his bed. He positions himself between my legs, and holding my knees, opens them for him.

He stares at my shaved pussy with a devilish smile, and before I can process what's happening, his mouth is on my clit, sucking.

I press my legs on his head, holding him in place while he keeps taking me closer to the best orgasm of my life.

His fingers press against my entrance while his mouth focuses on my clit, and he starts fucking me with his fingers.

I start shaking, unable to control my legs, as my orgasm approaches me.

Suddenly, he stops.

I groan in frustration, looking down at him.

"You know what to do," he says, his breath teasing my clit, but not enough to make me come.

My head speeds, trying to find what he's looking for. His words from earlier come back to me all of a sudden.

"I'm not gonna beg," I tell him, defiantly.

He gives me another devilish smile before returning his attention to my pussy. Every time his fingers enter me, he touches a soft spot that drives me insane with pleasure.

My climax approaches me fast again, and I moan.

Colton stops again.

I look down at him with a groan, desperate for my orgasm.

"Please, let me come. Just fuck me, please."

I ignore his pleased smile. I don't care if I just gave him what he wanted if that means I'm getting what I want too.

Colton finds a condom in his pockets and removes his clothes before getting between my legs.

His hard cock pressed against my entrance, entering me slowly, giving me time to get used to his invasion.

I'm so wet that he has a hard time controlling himself and not slamming down on me immediately.

When he's completely inside me, we both moan in pleasure while he starts moving in and out of me faster and harder.

My orgasm approaches me fast after all the teasing he did before, and I feel my pussy clench around his cock while I'm taken by the waves of pleasure.

He covers my mouth with his to muffle my scream, and pounds into me harder until he comes too with a roar.

Colton collapses on top of me, breathing hard. I hold him against my body for a while until he moves out of the bed to discard the condom.

"I should go," I tell him, getting dressed.

He looks at me with a serious expression. "I don't understand why you're with him."

I don't reply and leave the room. The truth is I don't know anymore either.

After a few weeks, I broke up with John. Colton and I lost contact. Until today. And he just asked me out.

Cheating on a Cheater

I've known my husband was cheating on me for months now. The late nights at work, the scent of cheap perfume, the unusual expenses.

At first, I was mad. After ten years of marriage, how could he do this to me? He's the only man I've ever been with. I gave him everything. And now he cheats.

I thought about confronting him, but when I asked about it, he just kept lying. He tied to fuck me that night. The first time he wants to have sex in over a year, and it's only to hide that he's having an affair.

I made up an excuse and left.

I'm gonna spend his money before his mistress does. The young man keeps showing me the newest shoes they have in store.

He's eager to make a sale and most of these shoes are worth more than I make in a week. I don't care. My husband can afford it.

As the young seller brushes my heel for the third time as he helps me try on the shoes, shivers run through me.

A thought crosses my mind, as I realize I have in front of me the perfect chance to get back to my husband. And I'm not talking about the shoes.

I open my legs a little and watch while the clerk glances up my dress, getting a good view of my panties.

The shoe in his hand falls to the ground, as he stares.

I bite my lower lip, smiling in what I hope is a sexy expression.

He looks up to me, his eyes meeting mine, and his cheeks turn bright red.

"Do you like what you see?"

He looks down, taking the shoe from the ground again, and helping me try it on.

"I'm sorry, I didn't want to stare," he says.

"Well, maybe that's what I wanted," I tell him, pressing my foot against his chest softly.

He glances up at my face before looking down at my foot. His hands caress my leg softly, tracing a path up my leg, to my knee, before going back down.

"Just keep going up," I tell him in a suggestive tone, opening my legs a little bit more.

He takes a look at my panties again before going caressing my leg again, but this time he reaches the aim of my dress before going down to my foot.

Unable to keep enduring his sweet torture, I stand, pushing him down on the floor with my foot.

He falls to the ground, looking at me in shock, as I pull my dress up to my waist and kneel on top of him, straddling him.

I feel the bulge of his hard cock against my wet pussy, and start grinding against him.

His hands caress my legs and my hips, pressing against me, making me moan with the contact.

I grab his hands, placing them on my breasts, and he feels my hard nipples through the fabric of my dress.

I'm glad I decided against a bra today.

The young man moves my dress down, revealing my breasts before his fingers start caressing my nipples, pinching them.

I moan as my head falls back with the pleasure he's giving me.

I reach down to his pants, unzipping them. I take his hard cock in my hands, stroking him softly, and feeling him against my pussy folds.

He leans into me, taking one of my nipples into his mouth, sucking and biting softly before running his tongue over the sensitive bud.

I keep stroking him, taking his balls in my hands, feeling their weight, and playing with them.

He moves his mouth to the other nipple, giving it the same attention he gave the first one. I moan, pressing against his mouth.

Suddenly, he moves away from my breasts, and holding me by the waist, makes me lay on the ground.

Before I can react, he opens my legs wide ripping my panties, and I feel his mouth against my clit, sucking.

I let out a strangled scream as he keeps teasing my pussy with his talented mouth, driving me closer to my climax.

My legs start shaking as he keeps fucking me with his tongue, but before I can reach the orgasm, he stops, pulling away.

I let out a groan in protest, but he ignores me, reaching for the back pocket of his pants.

I see that he's getting a condom, and wait patiently for him to cover himself before giving me what I desperately need.

He presses his tip against my pussy, entering me slowly, as I get used to his invasion.

When he's finally completely inside me, we both moan in pleasure before he starts moving in and out of me. His movements are slow and gentle at first, but as he starts approaching his climax, he starts thrusting into me faster and harder.

I move my hips to meet his rhythm, driven by the pleasure he's giving me.

I feel close to the orgasm again and reach down, caressing my clit in a circular motion, until I'm finally over the edge.

I drown in pleasure, my pussy clenching around his dick and taking him with me to the climax with a final thrust.

He collapses on top of me with a roar, his breath as fast as mine.

After a few seconds, he moves away from me, helping me stand before removing the condom.

I adjust my dress back in place, and take the ripped panties, shoving them into my purse.

He shows behind me, holding my hand and taking my panties from me before stoking them in his pants while I watch, surprised.

The door opens all of the sudden and an old lady enters the store. I realize that the door was open all along, meaning that anyone could have just entered and caught us fucking.

My cheeks burn, as I think how interesting that would be.

"I'm not sure if I should take them all today," I say, looking at all the shoes I've tried. "Or, maybe I should take just a pair today and come back later this week for more."

He gives me a smirk. "I think you should probably come back another day."

And that's exactly what I did. We never closed the door. The thrill of knowing at at any moment someone could just enter the store while we were fucking was the best part.

Fucking My Boyfriend's Brother

I can't believe the jerk cheated on me.

I pace on my living room, almost tripping on the table, as my eyes are glued on my phone.

I don't even know if he's aware that my cousin, Jenny sent me this.

My stomach turns, and I throw my phone into the couch.

The image of Jenny and Josh naked and in bed is burned in my mind, and I don't need to keep watching that.

A knock on the door startles me, and I take a deep breath. If this is Josh I might throw him down the stairs.

Jenny was almost like a sister to me, or that's what I thought. Looks like she doesn't feel the same about me.

I open the door to see Kevin, Josh's brother in front of me.

He looks concerned, which is weird on him. He's always been kind of a jerk to Josh and I, mostly when the two of us are together.

"What do you want?" I ask.

I don't have the patience needed to deal with his bullshit right now.

"How are you?" He asks.

I'm about to give him a snarky reply, but the concern in his eye stops me, making me wonder if he knows what's happening.

"Why?"

"I know Jenny sent you the pictures."

I take a deep breath, moving away from the door to let him in.

"How?"

"They were fighting. Josh was mad at Jenny, but she said that you deserve to know. I came over to make sure you're fine."

I get about a bottle of whiskey and some glasses for us.

I don't know for how long we drink or we talk, but I don't remember the last time we've spent this much time together. Especially without him being a jerk to me.

Turns out I actually like Kevin. He doesn't sound like a jerk anymore, but his brother just cheated on me with my best friend, so I guess he's just trying to solve his brother's problems.

"You know, it would be fun?" He asks with a devilish smile on his face.

I don't know if this the whiskey talking, but I had never noticed how attractive Kevin is until today. My heart beats fast as I turn to face him.

"What?"

"Well, maybe you could pay him with the same coin."

"What, like we should sleep together?" I ask, laughing.

He laughs too, but there's something in his eyes that tells me he wasn't joking. His smile vanishes and he stands.

"That wouldn't be a good idea, would it?"

I watch as he walks towards the door, ready to leave. We were having fun and suddenly, everything is over because something I actually want to do, even if it's not good or fair to none of us.

Kevin is about to leave and I need to make a decision fast.

My body reacts before I can think about what I'm doing, and I grab his arm right when he's about to open the front door to leave.

I make him turn around, pulling him into me and kiss his lips.

He seems surprised at first, but his hands pull me into him, resting on my back as he kisses me deeply. Our tongues dance together, exploring every corner of our mouths.

I moan against his lips, breaking the kiss.

He kisses a path down my neck, sending shivers through my body.

Kevin makes me turn around, pressing me against the front door as he presses against me.

I feel is hard cock on my stomach, and without a second thought, I reach out, stroking him through his jeans.

He groans, pressing against my hand.

"You're making me insane," he whispers in my hear, caressing my nipples through my shirt.

"Oh, God," I moan at his touch.

I keep stroking his cock, feeling him grow in my hands.

He pulls me to his arms, taking me to my bedroom, and throwing me into the bed.

I laugh, loving the desire in his eyes. no one as ever looked at me like that.

I pull my shirt through my head, seeing how his eyes turn into fire when he sees my naked tits.

I remove my shorts, laying in the bed wearing only my panties, as I wait for him to join me.

Kevin removes his clothes before kneeling down by my side on the bed.

He kisses my lips passionately.

"You're even more beautiful than I ever dreamed," he whispers against my lips before tracing a path of kisses down my body.

He takes one of my nipples into his mouth, sucking and licking the hard bud, and making me moan.

I arch my back, holding his head in place, I push him into me, as if if I'm afraid that he will stop at any moment.

He chuckles before turning his attention to the other nipple, giving him the same treatment.

Kevin goes down my body, kissing and licking my stomach, making me squirm.

He opens my legs, kneeling between them.

I hold my breath, looking down at him and watching as his head slowly approaches my pussy.

"Oh, fuck!" I moan, grabbing a handful of sheets.

His tongue runs across my folds, before he sucks my clit. He slips two fingers inside me, while his mouth keeps sucking and licking my clit.

I whimper as the climax approaches, while his fingers and his mouth keep their sweet turture to my body.

The waves of pleasure take over me, and I scream in pure ecstasies.

He moves up my body, taking a nipple into his mouth again, and I gasp, surprised with the pleasure I can still feel after that orgasm.

I push him into the bed, before straddling him.

He holds me on top of him, as I feel his hard cock pressing against my entrance.

I want him inside me, but I also wanna taste him so badly.

I lean forward, kissing him and stroking his hard cock, before moving down his body. I lick his tip, tasting him, and smile when he moans.

I take his dick into my mouth, sucking, while my hand moves up and down his wood at the same rhythm, before cupping his balls, caressing him.

He moves his hips, thrusting up slowly. I gag when he hits the back of my throat, and he tries to move away, but I keep trying to take him deeper into my mouth, gagging until my eyes become watery.

I move up his body, straddling him again.

Kevin pulls me for a kiss, while I adjust myself on top of him.

I slam down on him, taking him completely inside me with a single movement. We both moan, breaking the kiss.

He holds me by the hips as I star rocking on top of him, moving up slowly, just to slam down again, harder and faster.

I groan at the feeling of his cock stretching my pussy.

"You're so fucking tight," he whispers.

Suddenly, he grabs me by the waist, before rolling with me in the bed, so he's now the one on top.

Kevin takes one of my nipples into his mouth, sucking. He thrusts into me harder, and I let out a strangled scream, as pleasure takes over me again.

I hold on to his shoulders while he keeps sucking my nipple and thrusting into me faster and harder with every movement.

I move my hips to match his rhythm as the waves of pleasure run through my body.

My pussy clenching around his cock as I came take him over the edge and he comes inside me with a roar.

Kevin collapses on top of me, his breathing as erratic as mine.

After a couple of minutes, he moves away from me, pulling me against his body.

"Are you okay?" he asks.

I nod, smiling at him, and kissing him softly.

"I'm great," I pause for a couple of seconds. "Are you okay?"

He presses me against him, kissing my forehead.

"Yes. You have no idea for how long I've wanted this."

His words surprise me.

"Well, you've always been kind of a jerk to me, so I wouldn't know."

My phone interrupts us, as I get out of the bed to grab it.

I look at Kevin, my happiness suddenly vanishing.

"It's Josh."

I decline the call, sitting back on the bed.

"What do you wanna do?" Kevin asks, and I can see the pain in his eyes.

I take a deep breath.

"I don't know. The only thing I'm sure right now, is that I don't wanna see him or Jenny again."

"What about us?"

I shrug. "Maybe we can take things slowly from here, and see where that takes us?"

He nods, slowly, and his smile returns.

After I broke up with Josh, it took Kevin and I a couple of months to make things truly workout, but now, with our first baby about to be born, I know I made the right decision.

We might not have the best start, but we surely have a perfect happy ending.

My First Night with My New Boyfriend

Jaxson and I had been dating for a couple of weeks when I finally agreed to spend the night at his place.

He invited me to watch a movie, but I was so nervous about finally spending the night with him that I barely paid any attention to the movie.

My head rests against this chest as his hand caresses my arm softly. It's not a sensual gesture, but for some reason, that simple touch is enough to make my pussy wet.

I guess the anticipation wasn't helping either.

The movie ends, and Jaxson looks at me expectantly.

"What do you think?" He asks.

"Ah . . ." I look around, suddenly confused about his question. Did he ask something before that I didn't hear? "Oh! The movie! Right, it was great."

He smiles at me. "Did you fall asleep?"

I shake my head, embarrassed.

"It's okay if you did," he says in an amused tone. "I find that kinda cute."

I snort. "Cute? Right."

He nods. "It means you trust me enough to fall asleep in my arms."

My heart skips a beat at his words, and I feel my cheeks burn.

His words awake a desire in me that I never felt before, and I lean closer to him my lips brushing his.

"You're cute," I say against his lips.

With a groan, Jaxson pulls me to his arms, kissing me eagerly. I kiss him back with a passion that matches his, as his hands run across my back, pressing me against his muscular body.

We kiss for a long time, only stopping to catch our breath. His hands travel across my body, caressing every part of me that he can reach.

I run my fingers through his hair, pulling him into me as our tongues dance together, exploring and teasing for what's to come.

Breaking the kiss, Jaxson licks and nibbles my neck, kissing a path to my earlobe. When he reaches his destination, he sucks my earlobe into his mouth, biting me gently, and making me moan.

My hands travel down to his shoulders, feeling their strength as I caress his soft skin. It's amazing how something can be so strong and soft at the same time.

I pull his shirt by his head, and he helps me, before doing the same to me.

He looks at my bra with an amazing expression. "You're so beautiful."

His words make my heart skip a beat, as he pulls my bra to the side, revealing my head nipples.

His thumb brushes softly against my nipple, making me moan, before Jaxson leans forward, taking it into his mouth.

I moan, holding his head in place as he keeps teasing my breasts. He gives the other nipple the same attention, biting and sucking while the sensations run through me to my center of pleasure.

His hands unzip my jeans. He starts trying to pull them off, and when I feel him struggling, I lift my butt to help him out.

Jaxson takes the chance to pull my panties away along with my jeans, and I seat on his couch completely naked.

I reach to his jeans, but he holds my hand when I try to stroke his cock through the fabric. I look at him confused, but he just shakes his head with a devilish smile.

Opening my legs, he kneels between them, before caressing my pussy with his fingers.

"Fuck, you're so wet," he says, his thumb pressing on my clit.

"It's all for you, baby," I reply as my head falls back to the couch.

Jaxson starts caressing my clit in a circular motion before his fingers move down my folds to my entrance.

He slips two fingers inside me, at the same time his mouth replaces them on my clit. Sucking and licking me at the same time his fingers fuck me faster and deeper with every movement, Jaxson takes me to the verge of my orgasm.

I feel the waves of pleasure starting to grow, while his fingers press a sensitive spot inside me.

Suddenly, Jaxson stops his sweet torture on my body. Standing, he pulls me from the couch, as I whimper.

Jaxon makes me stand in front of him, kissing my lips before he makes me turn my back to him.

"Calm down, baby, I'll give you what you want," he says, pulling me onto the couch.

I kneel, supporting my hands on the back to the couch, and opening my legs for him.

I feel the tip of his cock against my entrance before he enters me with thrust, making us both moan.

He moves out of me almost completely just to thrust into me again, harder.

I gasp, his invasion giving me pleasure and pain at the same time as my pussy gets used to him.

He keeps fucking me harder and deeper with every movement. At some point I start pushing back and meeting his thrusts, matching his rhythm.

I feel close to the edge again, and my undoing comes when his fingers play with my nipples at the same time he thrusts into me.

My pussy clenches around his pulsating cock, taking him with me to the climax with a roar.

Jaxson collapses on top of me, holding me closer to him.

We're both breathing hard, and we lay on the couch together until our breath becomes normal again.

"That was amazing," he whispers on my hear.

I nod absently. All I can think about is how close he is to me, and how good he made me feel.

I want to do the same for him. Take him into my mouth until I'm gagging. Taste his cock. Play with his balls.

But first, we need to rest. Just a little. Before I leave tomorrow, I'll do all the things I want to do for him. I'll make sure this is just our first night together of many.

Turns out my wish came true, and we got to grow old together.

The Night I Got Home Late

It's been a couple of months since I got out with my friends. After my last breakup, the last thing I wanted was to go out, but my best friend wouldn't shut up, so here I am.

My mom had been calling me all night, ignoring that I'm twenty-two.

"Controlling boyfriend?" A male's voice sounds next to me.

I turn to face him. "Excuse me?"

He takes a seat next to me.

"I've been watching you all night, checking your phone and ignoring your calls," he pauses. "I just had to come over and tell you, that your boyfriend must be crazy if he doesn't trust you. But I must confess, if I were your boyfriend, my problem wouldn't be trusting you, but the guys that might approach you when you go out."

I laugh. "Like you?"

He leans forward. "Yes, just like me," he holds out his hand to me. "I'm Nick, by the way."

I take his hand in mine, giving him a handshake. "Jenny."

He holds my hand for longer than needed, caressing my soft skin, and sending shivers down my body.

I look at our hands, biting my lower lip.

Nick leans closer to me until I feel his breath on my neck.

"You shouldn't do that. It makes me want to bite your lips."

I feel my panties becoming wet at his words, and rest my hand on his leg.

"Well, maybe you should do it."

He looks at me surprised, before taking my lips with his, kissing me passionately.

I kiss him back, as my hand moves up his leg. I press my fingers against the bulge in his pants, and he groans against my lips.

His fingers move up my arm, resting on my shoulder and pulling me into him.

I keep stroking him through his pants, feeling him grow under my touch.

Suddenly breaking the kiss, he looks me in the eyes. We're both breathing hard from our kiss, and I smile.

"Maybe we should get out of here," he tells me. "I can't have you stroking my dick like that in a place where I can't eat your pussy."

I press my legs together as his words send shivers through me.

"Humm, when you put it like that, I can't refuse."

He follows me out of the bar. I wave goodbye at my friends, as I walk away.

I take him to my car, getting into the backseat.

I lay down, opening my legs to him. Nick lays on top of me, kissing me again.

His dick presses against my pussy, as he moves on top of me. My panties become damp at the contact and I let out a soft moan.

I reach for his jeans, unzipping them, and taking his cock in my hands, stroking him.

He breaks the kiss, groaning. His hands move down my body, and he unzips my jeans, slipping his fingers inside.

He finds my clit, moving his fingers in circles, taking me close to an orgasm.

I lift my ass, helping him remove my clothes before he gets his head between my legs.

"You smell so good," he says, licking my folds. "And you're so wet."

He licks me again, pressing his tongue on my clit, and teasing me. I hold his hair, keeping him in place as he keeps pleasuring me.

"Oh, God, yes, just like that, yeah!"

My orgasm takes over me, as waves of pleasure run through my body.

He lifts his head, kissing my stomach, before taking a condom from his jeans.

"You're so hot when you come, I can't wait to have felt you in my dick."

I watch as he covers his dick with the condom, before aligning himself between my legs.

I feel his tip against my entrance, and without any warning, he slams into me. I let out a moan, as my pussy gets used to his invasion.

He starts moving in and out of me, groaning as he speeds his rhythm, fucking me harder and deeper with every movement.

I feel a second orgasm approaching me again, as he lifts my shirt and takes a nipple into his mouth, sucking hard as his dick thrusts into me.

My pussy clenches around him as I come again, taking him closer to his climax.

"Oh, fuck, I'm coming!"

He slams into me one more time, as he reaches his orgasm, his fingers pulling me closer to him.

He collapses on top of me breathing hard, before moving away and discarding his condom.

I handle him a paper tissue from my purse, and he wraps the condom on it.

"Well, that was fun," he says, zipping his jeans.

I find my panties and my jeans and get dressed too.

My phone vibrates, and I check it to see that my mom is calling me again.

I accept the call, without looking at Nick.

"Yes, mom?" I ask in an annoyed tone.

"It's late, you should be home."

I sigh. "I'll be there in a couple of minutes."

I end the call before she can say anything else.

"Will I see you again?" Nick asks me, getting out of the car.

I shrug. "Maybe I'll call you next time I'm in town."

I drive away, without another word.

I did call him a couple of times until he decided to move closer. Soon, we were moving in together. Yesterday he proposed. I said yes, then I got on my knees.

Fucking the New Guy at the Office

I look at the newest addition to our team.

Thomas looks like a supermodel who got the wrong call for work. He's well built and muscular.

Every time I see him all I can think about is how I would like to throw him into the couch in the restroom and suck his cock.

I cross my legs, pressing them together as my pussy becomes wet with the image my mind is giving me.

How I would love to ride him on that damn couch, shove his face between my tits, and fuck him until we're both screaming with pleasure.

I've seen him looking at me, taking in my long legs as I wear the shortest skirts I can, trying to get his attention.

Not that getting his attention is hard. Being alone with him is what's been impossible.

Our team is working on a new project, and everyone has been working extra hours to make the deadline. I've been planning on a night out with some of my coworkers, trying to get a chance to get closer to Thomas, but until now I haven't been lucky.

It's already late at night when I walk out of my cubicle. The place is almost dark, and everyone left already.

When I'm about to get into the elevator, I hear someone singing.

I let out a chuckle, approaching the sound, curious to know who's the night singer.

I meet Thomas halfway back to the main area.

He immediately stops singing and dancing when he sees me, his cheeks bright red.

Fuck. He's adorable.

"Oh, Janet, sorry. I thought everyone had left already."

I shake my head. "Looks like we're the only ones left."

"Oh," he says, looking around.

Suddenly it hits me. We're the only ones left. This is my chance.

"I think I forgot my phone in the restroom. Do you mind helping me find it?"

He looks confused at first, but nods.

Thomas follows me to the restroom, and I feel his eyes on me as I move.

I unbutton my blouse slowly, making sure he doesn't know what I'm doing.

When we get to the restroom, I turn to face him with a smile, removing my blouse. I stand in front of me with only my lace bra covering my tits.

He stares at my breasts unable to look away, and I run my hands across my chest, pressing my boobs together.

"Do you like what you see?" I smile when he nods. "Don't you wanna come here and touch me?"

I reach for his hand and place it on my breasts.

He looks at me before focusing on my chest, slipping his fingers inside my bra and caressing my nipples.

Killing the distance between us, I pull him for a kiss, tasting the coffee on his lips.

He kisses me back eagerly, while his free hand pulls me into him. I feel his hard cock against my stomach and moan in anticipation.

Breaking the kiss, I shove him into the couch.

He looks at me expectantly, while I kneel next to him.

My hands caress his muscular body, unbuttoning his shirt slowly. I kiss his chest, tracing a path down his stomach, and lick his soft skin.

When I reach his pants, I unzip them, taking his big cock in my hands.

I hear him holding his breath as I run my tongue across his tip, tasting his salty pre-cum.

I take him into my mouth, sucking gently at first, while I stare at his expression. He closes his eyes, as his head falls back on the couch, lost in pleasure while I suck him.

My hands caress the base of his cock, moving to play with his balls as my head keeps bobbing up and down his length.

I keep trying to have him completely inside my mouth, but I end up gagging as he hits the back of my throat.

Thomas is lost in pleasure, moaning.

"Yeah, just like that, suck me," he whispers.

His words make me wet, and I slip a hand inside my skirt, playing with my clit in a circular motion while my mouth keeps sucking him.

"Everyone told me you liked sucking. I was starting to think I wouldn't have my turn."

Knowing that people in the office are talking about me makes me smile. Yes. I've fucked a couple of coworkers. But none of them has a cock as good as Thomas.

Moving away from his cock, I stand in front of him.

He looks at me with disappointment in his eyes.

I shrug. "You're right, I like sucking cock," I tell him removing my clothes slowly. "But I also like being properly fucked, and right now I want that cock inside me."

He smiles. "Sounds good to me."

I take a condom out of my bag and cover him slowly before sitting on top of him, straddling him.

I feel his cock against my pussy, and I grind on him, while he plays with my nipples.

He keeps caressing my nipple with his fingers while sucking on the other one.

I moan, my fingers slipping through his hair and pulling him closer to me.

He keeps sucking, licking, and biting my nipple until I'm whimpering before moving to the other to give it the same attention.

Reaching down between our bodies, I find his dick and positioning myself on top of him, I slam down on him.

He fills me, stretching my pussy.

We both moan in pleasure, as I give my cunt a couple of seconds to get used to his size before I start moving up and down his wood.

I slam on him faster and harder every time, and when I do, my clit pressed against his pelvis, taking me closer to an orgasm.

Having Thomas playing with my tits while I fuck him hard in the restroom, is too much for me.

I come with a scream, holding him by the shoulders as I try to support myself.

The waves of pleasure haven't subsided completely when he pulls me out of his lap.

Flipping me to my back, he makes me kneel on the couch, before aligning himself between my legs.

He enters me with a movement, fucking me deeper in this angle, and I moan as the pleasure returns.

"Oh fuck, yes! Fuck me hard!"

He holds me by the hips, thrusting into me harder and faster, in a rhythm almost impossible to follow.

"You feel so good on my cock," he says.

One of his hands moves up my body, grabbing my breast, and teasing my sensitive nipple.

I moan, the pleasure is almost unbearable.

His hand moves from my breast to my pussy.

When his thumb presses against my clit, I shatter in waves of pleasure, screaming.

"Oh god!"

My orgasm takes over me as I shake, unable to control my body's reactions.

My pussy clenches around his cock, until he comes too with a roar and a hard thrust into me.

"Oh fuck! Your pussy is milking me!" He says, his dick still inside me as my cunt keeps contracting around him.

Finally, the waves of pleasure start to subside and he moves out of me, collapsing on top of me.

I rest on the couch, still amazed by how he made me feel.

After a while, Thomas moves away from me, removing his condom and discarding it on a piece of paper before leaving it in the garbage.

I get up from the couch, collect my clothes, and get dressed slowly, suddenly unsure about what to say.

He gets dressed too, and I feel his eyes on me.

Taking a deep breath, I face him with a smile.

"Shall we go?"

He nods, resting his hand on my back and walking with me outside.

When it's time for us to say goodbye, we don't.

That night, Thomas went with me home. Then it was my turn to stay at his place.

Eventually, we got our place and moved in together.

The guys in the office had a hard time learning that now the only cock I would be sucking was Thomas', but with time someone else took my place as the office slut.

My Best Friend's Wedding

I glance at the other side of the aisle, where Jeffrey, the oldest brother of my best friend stands next to her fiancé.

She found the right man for her, and I'm happy to see her finally making it official at their wedding.

Jeffrey catches me staring at him, and winks at me with a devilish smile.

I bite my lower lip and look down at my feet, suddenly feeling my cheeks turning hot.

He always does this to me. He knows I've always had a crush on him, but all he's ever done was tease me.

But tonight things will be different. Tonight I have a plan to make things happen between us.

I'm done with him teasing me.

It's time for me to be the one teasing him, and leave him wanting more.

I face him again, and he's still looking at me. Running the tip of my tongue across my lips, I bite my lower lip gently before turning my attention to the bride.

I can feel his eyes on me, and I have to make an effort not to smile, or turn to face him again.

I want him to think that I'm no longer that into him. Maybe if he thinks he lost me, he'll realize he wants me.

Isn't that how it works in the movies?

The ceremony is finally over, and we follow the newly married couple to the club, where we're having dinner.

I got here with my best friend, but now she's leaving in her husband's car and I need to find someone else to take me to the club.

I watch along with all the other guests while the newly wedded couple leaves.

"So, so you need a ride?"

I turn and see Jeffrey a few inches away from me.

I look around, wishing I could just ride with someone else, but it looks like the other guests are already leaving.

I sigh, facing him again. There's a hint of a tease in his eyes, and I remember my plan.

"Sure, I would love to ride you," I reply, walking away from him without waiting to see his reaction.

He takes a couple of seconds to follow me into the parking lot, and I bite my lip to stop myself from smiling.

When I get to his car, I stare back at him, waiting while he approaches me with a possessed expression.

We get in the car at the same time.

I wait for him to get into the main road before checking him out. The bulge on his pants is visible.

"Maybe you should just stop and let me take care of that," I suggest, pointing to his pants.

"Fuck!" He whispers, glancing at me. "What's gone into you today?"

I give him an innocent smile. "What do you mean?"

He holds the wheel harder. "You know what I mean, you've been teasing me all day."

I lean closer to him. "Judging by what's in your pants I'm gonna guess you like it."

He glances at me again, his expression pained. "You're my sister's best friend."

I pull my skirt up to my legs, opening them wide as I slip a finger inside my panties.

"Yes, and I'm touching myself in your car, waiting for you to finally fuck me," I let out a soft moan when my fingers brush my clit. "What are you gonna do about it?"

I close my eyes as my fingers keep moving over my clit.

"Fuck, that's hot!" I hear him whisper while the car slows down.

I open my eyes to see that Jeffrey stopped in a reclusive area that can barely be seen from the road.

When I turn to face him, he pulls me into him, kissing me passionately.

I kiss him back, giving him access to my mouth and letting his tongue explore.

His hand replaces mine under my skirt. I open my legs wider, giving him better access while his fingers trace my folds.

I moan against his lips, as his fingers tease me, pressing against my clit.

I feel my orgasm close, my pussy so wet, that I wonder if I'm ruining my dress.

Jeffrey slips a finger inside me before two more join the first while he keeps teasing my clit with his thumb.

His mouth travels down my neck, licking and kissing my sensitive skin, sending goosebumps through my body.

Waves of pleasure run through my body, taking me high as my orgasm hits me.

Jeffrey removes his hand from my skirt, leaning back into his seat as I look at him still amazed by how he made me feel.

I see him adjusting his pants over his cock, and without a second thought, I reach out for him.

Jeffrey looks at me surprised, as I unzip his pants and take his dick in my hands, stroking him gently.

Leaning forward, I lick his tip already leaching pre-cum, before taking him completely in my mouth, sucking.

I do my best to give him the best blowjob of his life, licking, sucking, and stroking him as best as I can.

He rests his hand on my head, caressing my hair and pulling me into him as my mouth keeps sucking me.

Jeffrey thrusts harder and faster, his tip hitting the back of my throat and making me gag.

Suddenly moving me away from his cock, Jeffrey readjusts his seat before pulling me into his lap.

I sit on top of him, straddling him. His wood brushes my pussy as I move on top of him.

He moves my dress down, revealing my hard nipples, needing attention.

I let out a moan when he pulls one of my nipples into his mouth, sucking and biting gently before moving to the other one and giving it the same attention.

Unable to keep holding out, I reach down between our bodies and taking him in my hand, I hold his cock against my entrance as I go down on him slowly.

I feel his sick stretching my pussy as I keep moving, trying to get used to his size.

I whimper when I feel him completely inside me, and I wait for a couple of seconds before moving up.

I slam down on him, this time harder, and we both moan.

Jeffrey holds me by the hips, thrusting into me, and helping me find the rhythm that'll take us both to the climax.

I keep moving on top of him, his pelvis pressing against my clit every time k move, taking me closer to the orgasm.

When he takes my nipple into his mouth again, sucking hard, at the same time I slam on him, the waves of pleasure take over me again, this time in the strongest orgasm I've ever felt.

I scream in pleasure, unable to stop myself, while the pleasure keeps growing, in an orgasm that feels eternal.

Finally, Jeffrey thrust into me one last one, coming too with a roar.

I collapse on top of him while he rests his head on my shoulder, both of us breathing hard.

I smile as I move away from him. I don't know for how long we've been like this, but I know soon his sister will be looking for us.

He looks confused at first as if he wants to hold me forever, and my heart skips a beat at the thought.

"Sasha will be looking for us soon," I tell him.

He nods, adjusting his clothes as I do the same.

"You're right. We should be going," he starts the engine and drives us to the party.

We avoid each other the rest of the night, as we're both afraid of how Sasha would react if she knew what happened between us.

Later that night, Jeffrey knocked on my hotel room door.

We spent the night together, and every night after that.

Tonight, we're the ones getting married.

Naughty New Year's Eve With My Stepdad

I knock on his door, the people inside partying so loud that I doubt he can even hear me.

Luckily for me, he does.

His eyes immediately light up when he sees me standing at his door, at least for a few seconds. Until he sees the backpack at my feet.

"What happened?" He asks, grabbing the backpack and taking it inside.

I follow him, shrugging, even though he can't see me doing it as he's taking me to one of the bedrooms.

"She got a new husband. He's an old dude full of money. She says I'm tempting him, so I decided to leave before shit hits the van."

He doesn't look surprised. Married to mom for only a few months, Jensen got his divorce the moment my mom realized he didn't have as much as she thought.

He's much closer to my age than all other guys she's ever married. We ended up staying in contact and we became friends.

He opens the door to one of the guest rooms. This isn't the first time I've slept here.

"You know where everything is, right?"

I nod.

"I have a New Year's Eve party, as you've noticed. You can join us if you want."

I look down at the bed before I stare at his amazing eyes. I know what I want and it isn't to join his guests.

I want him. I've wanted him for a long time now, and all that's stopped me from making a move is my fear of how he might react.

But tonight I don't care.

My mom just made me leave the house I was born in because she was afraid of her husband's interest in me.

My life will never be the same.

What do I have to lose?

I take a step closer to him, resting my hand on his chest. I look up at him in what I hope is a seductive expression.

"I think I want to stay here," I tell him. "Will you stay with me?"

He looks at my hand, before glancing at the closed door.

"Trish ..."

I see the doubts in his eyes and decide to take things a little farther.

Stepping on my tiptoes, I kill the distance between us and press my lips against his.

He doesn't react.

I move away from him, my cheeks burning.

"Oh, shit, I'm sorry," I start. "Please don't make me leave. I don't have anywhere to go."

He looks puzzled for a few seconds, standing still for a few seconds.

Suddenly, he kills the distance between us and takes my lips with his, kissing me with a passion that matches mine.

My hands run across his body, feeling his muscular arms and shoulders through the fabric of his clothes like I've dreamed for a long time.

I can't believe this is happening.

His hands pull me closer, resting on my waistline. His fingers slip under my shirt, caressing my soft skin, sending shivers down my body.

I press closer to him, feeling the bulge of his already hard cock against my stomach.

Reaching down between our bodies, I stroke his dick through his jeans. He groans and presses himself against my hand.

I unzip his jeans and pull them down enough to free his meat, feeling his skin on my hands.

I stroke him gently.

He breaks our kiss and traces a path down my neck, licking and nibbling my sensitive skin until he finds my chest.

I move a few inches to give him space to remove my shirt. He pulls my bra down enough to show my tits, and leaning down, pulls a hard nipple into his mouth.

He sucks, bites, and licks my nipples until I'm moaning and pressing against him.

The pleasure he's giving me is almost unbearable.

My panties are drenched, and I press my legs together, trying to make it better, even if I know that the only way this ache will pass is with his cock inside me.

He unzips my jeans, and pulls them down along with my panties, throwing them on the floor. My bra follows the same destination.

He pulls me into the bed, making me lay down on my back.

"Are you sure about this?" He asks, his hand on his jeans.

I nod. How can he ask me this?

"I need you inside me."

My words are like a trigger for him. He removes his jeans, and lays on top of me, adjusting himself between my legs.

I feel the tip of his cock against my wet pussy, making me moan in anticipation.

He takes a nipple into his mouth again, at the same time he guides himself to my entrance.

His cock enters me slowly, stretching my pussy in a pleasure that I can barely take.

When he's completely inside me, we both moan before he starts moving in and out of me in a rhythm that takes us to the climax.

When his orgasm approaches, he starts pounding into me faster and harder.

One of his hands slips between our bodies. He finds my clit and strokes it, taking me over the edge.

My strangled scream takes him to the climax and he comes inside me with a groan.

He pounds into me one last time, before he collapses on top of me, breathing hard.

I can't stop smiling when he moves away to look at me.

"Are you okay?" He asks, his voice full of concern.

I nod eagerly.

"I'm perfect. You have no idea for how long I wanted you."

He looks down. "Maybe for as long as I've wanted you."

I press against him, my body completely relaxed against his.

Downstairs we hear his guests counting down to midnight.

"Happy new year," he says in my ear, kissing me softly.

I smile.

This is the best way to start the new year. And the next one for as long as I'm alive.

My Cousin Fucks Me Right On The Beach

Having a house on the beach is the best. That means that every year when the weather allows it, my family comes to visit, and I get to see Phil.

Okay. The house isn't mine.

It belongs to my stepdad.

Phil is his nephew, and that means that my mom keeps insisting that I should call him cousin.

I don't care.

All I care about is seeing his perfect body in his bathing suit.

I look at him while he approaches me, his body wet as he just got out of the ocean.

"Why won't you join me in the water?" He asks, sitting next to me on my towel.

I shrug.

"I'm kinda busy right now. But thanks."

He glances at the book next to me.

"Yeah. I saw you were busy. Watching me."

I gasp.

I hadn't realized I was that obvious.

"I—"

I look down, my cheeks burn with embarrassment.

A movement next to me startles me, and I look up, wondering if he's leaving. To my surprise he's a few inches away from me, his face so close that if I move just a little I'll be tasting his lips.

His hand caresses my hair softly, locking it behind my ear. I watch while his muscles move.

"You're so cute," he says under his breath.

I bite my lower lip. All I want right now is to kiss him, but I've already made a fool of myself today. What if he doesn't kiss me back?

My mind stops wondering when he's the one killing the distance between us. He kisses me passionately, making me moan. Taking advantage of the opening, he slips his tongue into my mouth, exploring.

Shivers run through my body while he pulls me closer to him.

My hand caresses his arms and shoulders, feeling his muscles contract under my touch, and I wonder how amazing it must be to taste his skin salty from the sea.

He makes me lay on the towel, while he lays on top of me. I feel his hard cock pressing against my stomach.

Without thinking, my hand travels down his chest, finding the aim of his swimsuit. I caress his dick through the fabric, feeling it harden at my touch.

He moans softly, pressing himself against my hand. Phil's mouth leaves mine, tracing a path down my neck. He nibbles and kisses my soft skin before giving me gentle bites. I close my eyes, throwing my head back, giving him better access.

His hand caresses my breast through the thin fabric of my bikini. A low moan escapes my lips when he pinches my nipple.

Tired of feeling him with the barrier of his swimsuit, I manage to pull his clothing down enough to finally free his cock.

I stroke him gently, amazed by his size. Cupping his balls, I caress them with my fingers, feeling their weight.

I can't wait to have him inside me, but it looks like Phil has other plans.

Pulling my bikini top to the side, he feels my hard nipples with the tip of his fingers before he takes on with his mouth.

I moan my free hand on his hair, pulling him closer to me.

After giving the same attention to the other nipple, he keeps going down my body, until he's kissing my bikini bottoms.

Goosebumps run through my body when he unties the bikini, removing the fabric and revealing my shaved pussy.

The hot air caresses my skin before he kisses my pussy.

I open my legs wider, giving him better access to my entrance.

He licks me from my entrance up to my clit before focusing his attention on my needy bud. His fingers find my entrance too and he slips two fingers inside me, moving in and out.

I'm about to reach the climax when I pull him aside and make him lay on the towel, I sit on top of him, straddling him.

The tip of his dick presses against my entrance, and I use his shoulders as support and lower myself on his cock.

He enters me slowly, while my wet pussy gets used to his invasion. When he's finally completely inside me we both moan.

I move up before slamming down on him. He holds me by the hips and helps me establish a rhythm that will take us both over the edge.

I speed up, slamming down on him harder, feeling how my clit presses against his pelvis every time he's balls deep inside me.

The pressure finally sends me over the edge. I bury my face on his shoulder to muffle the scream of pleasure that runs through me while I ride my orgasm.

He follows me to the climax thrusting into me hard a few more times. Phil collapses on the towel, taking me with him.

I rest my head on his chest, feeling his heartbeat as fast as mine.

His hand caresses my back gently and I smile.

After a while, I move away from him and adjust my bikini to cover my body again.

He does the same with his swimsuit before he finally faces me.

"That was—never in my wildest dreams could I have imagined this," he says, shaking his head.

I smile. "I'll take that as a compliment." Then his words sink in. "You've dreamed about me?"

He nods. "I've had a crush on you since the first time we've met."

My smile gets bigger. "That's cute."

He shrugs. "Don't make fun of me."

My expression becomes immediately serious. "No. I'm not making fun of you. I would never do that," I make a pause. "I couldn't because I've had the biggest crush on you too. This is like a dream come true for me."

We walked into the house together, holding hands. We found a way to be alone as much as possible without anyone suspecting what was going on between us.

Eventually, we decided it was time to be in the clear with our relationship. We got married. Today is our firstborn birthday.

My Stepson Comforts Me

Ladies, be advised: if the man you're marrying is already divorced a couple of times, nothing stops him from replacing you too when he gets tired of you.

That's what happened to me.

My marriage lasted three years. I was his fifth wife. He already had an adult son from his first wedding.

Robert is the only reason my marriage lasted that long.

He's sensitive, attractive, and always worried about my needs. Sometimes I wished I had met him first.

A knock on my door startles me, and I jump out of my seat.

Opening the door, I see Robert staring at me with worried eyes.

"Damn, Jen, you can't just open the door like that! What if someone wants to hurt you?"

I shrug. "You're overreacting, Rob."

I move away from the door to let him into my small apartment.

Moving out of his father's mansion and into this small place on the bad side of town was a shock, but I know I'm better off now.

He looks around the place, taking in the stained couch.

"I already clean it, but I'll need to find something to cover that," I tell him, suddenly embarrassed.

He looks at me, running his hands through his air.

"You shouldn't be here. Why can't you come and stay with me?"

He invited me several times. Problem is, I don't know if I'll be able to resist my feelings if we're living together.

"I—I can't. Thanks. This is best for everyone."

Rob approaches me, holding me by the arms and making me face him. Electricity runs through my body as he touches me, and I almost melt against him.

"Jen, please, I can't let you do this."

I take in his pleading look, and my eyes linger on his lips, wondering how good he must taste.

His eyes travel down my face, stopping at my breasts, and watching while I take a deep breath.

"Jen . . ." He whispers, leaning closer to me.

I lick my lips, trying to remember why we shouldn't do this, but my mind went blank, and all I can think about is how much I want him.

"We can't," I whisper, but my head moves on its own, almost killing the distance between our lips.

He brushes his lips on mine. "Why not? I know you want me as much as I want you. Don't you wanna feel me inside you?"

I whimper at his words. He knows me too well.

I take a deep breath, trying to clear my mind and decide what to do, but instead, I end up killing the short distance between our lips, taking his mouth with mine.

He pulls me closer to him, kissing me deeply as his hands run across my body.

I feel his hard cock against my stomach, and let out a small whimper while my hands travel down his chest to the bulge on his pants.

He breaks the kiss when I caress him through his clothes, moaning softly.

My pussy is already wet in anticipation of what's to come.

Robert pulls me towards the couch, making me lay there, while he kneels between my legs.

Leaning forward, he kisses me again passionately, our tongues dancing together while he presses his cock against my pussy.

I moan again, lost in the pleasure he's giving me.

I always knew we would be a good match but this is so much better than I expected. I can't believe how he's making me feel.

Pulling my shirt through my head, I lay on the couch with a pink bra.

Robert looks down at my chest, taking in the views before his eyes meet mine with a smile.

"They're even better than I had fantasized," he tells me, removing the bra.

I want to ask him about his fantasies, but all words disappear when his mouth finds my nipple.

Robert sucks, licks and nibbles the small bud while his hand caresses the other one.

I hold his head in place, pulling him closer to me, while I moan. My head falls back, and I press myself against his cock, needing to feel more.

He moves to the other nipple, giving it the same attention as the first one. His hand moves down to my shorts, unbuttoning them.

I gasp when his fingers slip inside my panties, feeling my folds, and teasing my entrance before coming back to my clit, caressing me in a circular motion.

"Fuck, you're so wet," he whispers against my nipple, kissing down my stomach.

I help him remove the remaining clothes I'm wearing until I'm completely naked in front of him.

"I've dreamed about this for so long," he says, holding me by the knees and opening my legs to give him access to my cunt.

I let out a strangled scream as his tongue runs across my folds, pressing against my entrance.

He moves up again, finding my clit, licking. gently at first. Robert keeps eating my pussy eagerly, as my legs start shaking with the approach of my orgasm.

My hands run through his hair, and I hold him in place while he slips two fingers inside me.

"Oh, please, just—," I don't finish the sentence as my orgasm hits me in waves of pleasure.

He slows down his rhythm, moving his tongue away from my sensitive clit, and licking my juices from his fingers.

"You're so hot when you come," he says.

I open my eyes to see him removing his pants and taking a condom from his pocket.

"Now I want to see you cum in my cock," he says, adjusting himself between my legs.

I feel his tip pressing against my entrance as he slowly moves inside me.

I let out a small moan as his dick stretches my pussy, and he enters me completely.

We both gasp at the sensation, and he kisses me softly before he starts moving out of me just to slam back.

"Oh fuck."

Robert starts moving faster, thrusting into me harder with every movement. Our moans of pleasure fill the place, and I wonder if the neighbors can hear us through the thin walls.

Robert moves out of me and makes me kneel on the couch before he slams on me again from behind.

In this position, he goes deeper inside me, and I scream at the feeling of him inside me.

"Yes, harder! Faster!" I beg him.

This seems to take away the little control he had, as he starts pounding me harder and faster with every movement.

His hand finds my clit and he caresses me, taking me closer to the orgasm. the waves of pleasure take over me again, and I come with a strangled scream.

He moves away from me, and I turn to him, taking his cock in my hands. I remove the condom, and he looks at me, surprised.

"I want you to come in my mouth."

I stroke him as fast as I can before I take him into my mouth.

I take him as deep as I can, until his tip hits the back of my throat, making me gag.

He holds my head in place, as he thrusts into my mouth, my eyes full of tears as I struggle to breathe.

Robert lets go of my head, and I take a deep breath, letting my hands play with his balls.

I lick his tip, before going down on him again.

"I'm cumming!" He says at the same time his load fills my mouth.

I swallow, but his load was so big that some of it runs down my chin.

I smile and move away from his cock, I use my fingers to clean my hub before licking them.

Robert looks at me, breathing hard.

"Fuck, that was hot," he tells me, pulling me closer to him.

I rest my head against his chest, hearing his heartbeat.

I'm not sure about what this means to us, but it doesn't matter. Not right now. All I care about now is how he made me feel.

What the future holds, can be argued later.

But I'm case you want to know, we kept seeing each other for a couple of months before we decided to become exclusive.

When his family found out about our relationship, they didn't take it well, as it was expected.

Robert turned his back to them for me. We married four years ago. His family is slowly accepting our relationship.

He stills fuck me like no one else. Maybe another time I can tell you about that night on the beach. Or our wedding night.

Or all the other times I'll never forget.

I Found Myself a Vampire to Fuck

I've been told several times during my life that the best fuck a woman can have is a vampire.

Obviously, they're not easy to find, but this time I feel lucky.

My friend told me about this underground club where all supernatural species like to hang out.

The bouncer gave me a pitying look when he saw me with my almost too short red dress.

I don't care about his judgment. I got here to find myself a vampire, and I'll only leave when I get to fuck one.

The dance floor is full of people and I manage to walk to the center, where everyone can see me.

I move my body to the rhythm of the music. It doesn't take long before someone is behind me, dancing.

I turn to face him. My heart skips a beat. His pale skin tells me what I needed to know.

I got what I wanted. I got myself a vampire's attention.

We keep dancing through the night.

His hands rest on my hips while we dance.

I grind my ass against him, feeling his hard cock press against me.

He kisses my neck from behind, giving me gentle bites. Goosebumps run through my body with the simplest of touches from him.

"Wanna go somewhere else?" He asks in my ear.

I glance back at him, nodding with a smile.

He holds my hand, taking me outside.

Down the street, in a dark parking lot, we find his car.

He opens the door for me, but I shake my head and get on the back seat.

I don't know where he wants to take me, but I can't wait anymore.

He shrugs before getting into the back with me.

"I'm—"

I lean into him, taking his lips with mine, interrupting him.

He's frozen for a few seconds but then kisses back with passion.

My hands travel across his body, feeling his muscular body.

His hand slips up my leg, caressing my soft skin. I open my legs for him, granting him access to my pussy.

His fingers feel me through the thin fabric of my lace panties and I moan against his mouth.

Our tongues dance together in a rhythm that mimics the one our bodies desperately need.

I reach down to his pants, stroking his hard cock with my fingers before unzipping them. I take him in my hand, feeling his soft skin between my fingers.

His fingers move my panties to the side, feeling my folds. I moan again, my head falls back on the seat.

He presses his thumb against my clit, caressing me softly in circles. Two of his fingers press against my entrance. I moan again when he starts fucking me with his fingers at the same time he teases my clit.

I keep stroking his hard cock, playing with his balls, feeling their weight in my hand.

He kisses my neck, going down to my cleavage. He moves my dress down, revealing my breasts. I'm not wearing a bra, and he takes a nipple into his mouth while he keeps his wonderful teasing to my pussy.

I moan loudly, losing control of my own body. I shake in his arms when the orgasm hits me and I feel like I'm flying.

Before I have time to come down from my orgasm, he adjusts our bodies in the back seats so I'm laying back. He gets between my legs, opening them and pressing the tip of his cock against my entrance.

He keeps teasing me, entering me slowly.

Unable to keep waiting, I reach down to his hips and pull him closer to me, making him slam into my body.

We both moan in pleasure. My eyes stay glued to his while he starts moving in and out of me, slowly at first, but speeding his rhythm every time he thrusts into me.

I move my hips to his encounter, making him fuck me deeper and harder.

He leans closer to me, taking a nipple into his mouth again and sucking.

A gasp escapes my lips when I realize I'm close to another orgasm.

Suddenly, he stops.

I look at him confused, needing the release I know is coming.

Moving out of me, he makes me change in the seat until I'm on all fours.

He caresses my back softly until he reaches my cunt, running his fingers through my folds.

His dick presses against my entrance again. Without a warning he slams into me, harder and deeper in this position.

I let out a strangled scream while he keeps moving in and out of me.

His hand slaps my ass hard before he caresses the stinging spot gently.

I scream, a mix of pleasure and pain.

Suddenly he pulls me closer to him until o have my back against his chest. He starts kissing my neck at first.

I close my eyes.

I feel a sharp pain when his teeth bite my neck, but somehow the pain vanishes while he keeps his mouth glued to the sensitive area.

When he reaches down to my clit to stroke it slowly, my orgasm hits me again, sending me flying in waves of pleasure.

He pulls me forward again, moving away from my neck, and holding me by the waist, thrusts into me a few more times until he comes inside me with a roar.

I collapse on the seat. He stays unable to move for a few minutes.

When I finally move, I see him staring at my neck.

"Sorry," he says. "I got carried away."

I touch the pained area and my fingers found something moist. Blood.

I shrug.

"It's okay," I tell him, adjusting my clothes back to place.

I can't tell him that this is what I was looking for. I wanted a vampire. To fuck. And I know what that means.

I don't mind if he feeds on me, for as long as I keep having the best sex of my life.

Want to read more steamy short stories for free? Click here to get free access to the first few stories I wrote in 2022 plus the stories I wrote for other Medium publications during 2021.

OTHER BOOKS BY THE AUTHOR

Liah Wilder publishes mostly on her profile on Medium. If you like her work, please check out her other stories there, and follow her profile.

Want to check out her other published stories? Click here to see all available stories in the store.

Ingram Content Group UK Ltd.
Milton Keynes UK
UKHW011836190323
418793UK00004B/498